The Demon King's
Healer
EverEri

CONTENT WARNING

The content in this book may not be suitable for everyone. Please be aware that this book contains the following:

Explicit sex scenes
Darker themes

To Samantha Thomas, my favorite vampire with the most healing hugs.
And to those who would sacrifice yourself for your friends. You deserve just as much love as you give to the world.

Chapter 1

*W*hat the fuck?

I dangled in the air, caught in a net made of thick rope with no idea how I got into the mess. I had left my room for a simple stroll, and the hallway had been seemingly empty, as it usually was in the middle of the night. Most of the residents at the demon king's estate tucked themselves away to ignore the strange sounds that echoed in the shadows at night. The noises didn't bother me. I was a creature of the night, and I found solace in the dark.

Not getting caught in traps.

What the actual fuck?

There was no reason for a random net to be in the hallway of the estate. All I had to do was slice through the rope with my nails. My vampiric nature made me stronger than most of the other beings in the estate, but I didn't want to mess up my perfect manicure. Instead, I looked for the mechanism holding up the net. A single rope was attached to the ceiling, and my weight pulled the opening shut.

I had two choices.

Squirm to try to free myself or risk messing up my nails.

1

I flicked out my nails, taking a moment to look at dark red drips painted by an artist's hand. With a simple swipe, a piece of rope snapped. I took my time, but that only increased my frustration. If I ever found out who set this net up—

"It looks like I caught a little vampire in my trap tonight." A lilting voice echoed against the empty halls, grating my nerves from the delight in her delicate voice. Whoever it was took pleasure in my dismay.

I twisted my body in an unnatural position, catching a glimpse of the woman standing beneath me. She rested her head on the end of a scythe, looking up with glowing green eyes. Her pink and purple hair lay in waves over her shoulders, humidity adding volume. Her mouth stretched into a smile filled with gleam.

I had never seen her at Ethlow before, and I knew all the residents at the demon king's estate. As the only healer at Ethlow, everyone came to me sooner or later, and I had connections with those in charge, so I was one of the first informed of any newcomers.

"Who are you?" I tried to sound commanding, but my voice came out higher pitched than intended. It was the fake voice I used with most residents.

She pushed her hair behind pointed ears, revealing several silver piercings. "You're kind of cute." She winked and giggled, not taking me or the situation seriously.

"This isn't funny. Let me down."

"Rawr!" She curled her fingers in the air like a claw. "She's feisty!" She stood and flipped her scythe into the air. In a wide sweeping motion she slashed the weapon towards me. I flinched, but the blade hit the rope above the net. The next second, I was falling. My lithe body twisted, landing on my feet with grace. It was one of the advantages of a vampire's immortal body.

I yanked the rope off me and tossed it to the side. I faced the stranger, not bothering to hide my scowl. "Who do you think you are?" Either she didn't realize she was in the demon king's estate, or she didn't care. "You can't just set traps in Zathrian's estate. If Viridian discovered you, he'd probably kill you."

I didn't know why I bothered to give her a warning after she trapped me. For all I knew, she was here to hurt the demon king or the residents. The people I cared about most lived at the estate, and I couldn't afford to let a threat walk free.

Those who showed up at Ethlow asking for asylum didn't do so because they thought it was fun. Most of us ended up in the haunted estate because there was nothing left for us in the outside world. The last thing any of us needed was an intruder setting traps.

The stranger tilted her head, unphased by my warning. "Zathrian? You mean King Zathrian, one of the five demon kings?"

I didn't respond, unsure of where she was going. It was clear she knew exactly where she was, but she had yet to reveal if her intentions were nefarious.

She walked around me, circling me like a vulture. I stood straight, refusing to back down. "What does it matter to you?"

"I'm just surprised you speak about the demons at this estate with such fondness. Most beings curse demons—even many

3

demons themselves." Her scythe glinted, reflecting a source of light invisible to my eyes. I watched her weapon closely. If she decided to attack, and I wasn't prepared, she could do serious damage.

I twisted my body, following her closely as she circled round and round. "There are some demons who take advantage of others, but it's not like that here. I would be careful if I were you. The master of the house does not take threats to the estate lightly. If he finds you breaking in—"

She stopped walking, a giggle taking over her features. "Don't worry, little vampire. I am beyond the touch of the demon kings of the realm. I answer to a higher power."

Strange magic flowed from her, one I wasn't familiar with. I had tasted the magic of witches, demons, and even fae, but she belonged to none of them. "Who are you?"

In the blink of an eye, she disappeared, reappearing on the ceiling. "I am the grim reaper of Kinzlea, and I have come to Ethlow for a visit. But you, Satella, you may call me Astoria."

I stumbled back. I had read about grim reapers, but in the centuries I had been alive, I had never met one. "But you don't look like a grim reaper." I had seen dozens of drawings, and they were all the same, black hooded figures with shadows hiding the face of the being.

Astoria flipped from the ceiling to the floor, using some sort of transportation magic. She tugged at her frayed black skirt that was cut down to her upper thighs. The lower half of her shirt was missing, showing her midsection. "I know. The standard uniform is just so drab. If I'm going to handle death, I'm going to handle it my way."

I stumbled back, my stomach twisting. My fangs extended as my mouth dried out. I was painfully familiar with death. As an immortal, I had suffered through the deaths of friends and family I cared for. As a vampire, I had been the cause of too many deaths that continued to haunt me. As a healer, I had seen far more deaths than I ever wanted to admit. I wanted to heal others to make up for mistakes I had made, but it didn't always work in my favor.

I *fucking* hated death.

The grim reaper was a reminder of those failures. It was as if the universe was taunting me by putting the symbol of death inches away from me.

"You're not welcome here." I didn't want Astoria to see the fear that crept through my spine. "Leave now."

Astoria's eyes flickered yellow. "Shame. I thought maybe we could be friends. Guess I'll have to find someone else to show me around." She disappeared as quickly as she appeared.

The pounding in my head was the only sound in the hollow hallway. I pressed my hands against my chest, willing my muscles to relax.

Death was roaming the halls of the demon king's estate. What the fuck was I supposed to do?

Chapter 2

T he breeze shifted from warm summer air to the chill of fall. The change of season was fully in effect, which meant I had weeks at best before the air turned cool and dry, making my joints ache. Biologically, I should've hated the summer and the sun. It weakened vampires, making them vulnerable to attacks. I didn't have to worry about that at Ethlow. Between the demon king, the master of the house, and the guardsmen, the estate was one of the most protected places in all of Kinzlea.

I preferred feeling weak to feeling the ache in my joints that came with winter. I intended to spend as much time outside as possible, knowing the heat could disappear overnight with the temperamental autumn air.

The door opened and closed, bringing three sets of steps with it. I spent most afternoons with my two closest friends, Aukina and Nyri. They had been at the estate a fraction of the time I had been, but they were skilled at finding trouble and boyfriends. It was often the same thing.

"Satella, you're surprisingly early," Aukina said. Her hand was linked with Reamann's, one of the demon guards. Ever since the two of them started copulating, they were practically inseparable, unlike Nyri and her mate. Nyri was dating the demon king, who had a lot more responsibilities to keep him busy. He rarely joined us for our daily meal.

I looked at the orange-haired demon and narrowed my eyes. "You. Leave." I motioned for Reamann to go anywhere else.

He lifted his eyebrows, making the mistake of challenging me. "Why should I leave?"

"Because you're a man, and I don't feel like talking to you." I crossed my arms, holding firm. The fewer people around, the better. The topic I wanted to discuss with my friends wasn't something I wanted to get around. I knew Nyri would likely tell her mate later, especially since the safety of the estate was his responsibility, but I didn't care—as long as he wasn't present for this discussion.

Aukina placed her hand on Reamann's chest. She was the opposite of the demon in almost every way. She was shorter than him by more than a head. Her hair was as dark as the night with a new moon. She was round and fluffy with beautifully tanned skin. The mermaid had an elegance to her that came from her royal upbringing.

Reamann, on the other hand, was tall, pale, and had burning orange hair.

"It's okay," Aukina said. "I'll see you after dinner." As the cook in charge of the kitchen, her work was rarely done, but she resigned to stop after the dinner rush.

Reamann grimaced, not bothering to hide his annoyance. I winked at him, rubbing it in. He bared his canines at me, and I flipped him off. It was all fun and games. I wasn't really mad at him, and he was just sad he couldn't spend every moment with his mermaid lover. It was good for the couple to spend time apart, though.

Once Reamann was gone, Nyri turned to me. "I'd ask if you slept enough, because you seem cranky, but you don't sleep."

I sat on the patch of grass in the private courtyard. The ground used to be covered in dirt, but Nyri's magic was attuned to plants. She had made the courtyard less desolate by tending to the grass, and bringing to life the tree that provided us shade.

I waited for the others to sit before I began. They both chose the shade of the tree, opposite to my spot in the sun. They didn't touch their food, waiting for me to find the words to describe my need for privacy.

"I got caught in a trap last night." I glanced at my nails, re-membering how the situation had messed them up. It made my irritation resurface, but I quickly pushed it back down.

Nyri blinked three times. "Is that some sort of euphemism?"

"No. I was on my nightly walk, and then suddenly I was dan-gling in the air in a rope net." I had to pause, feeling my temper rise. I didn't want my friends to see that side of me. I didn't want to let the grim reaper get to me.

"I don't understand," Nyri said.

"Was this a prank from Malse? Reamann says the goblin likes to play pranks," Aukina added.

I paused, not ready to tell them about the grim reaper. I wanted to ask them why they thought she'd show up at the demon king's estate, but there only seemed to be one logical answer—one that made my stomach roil.

"It was someone I hadn't met before. She said she was visiting the estate." *And that she was a grim reaper.* "But I wasn't aware of anyone visiting. Maybe Zathrian would know who she is." I looked at Nyri. Having a friend dating the demon king had its perks.

"He hasn't said anything," Nyri said. She played with her golden brown hair. "But I can ask him. He would know if there was a guest or a new resident."

Not if Astoria was truly a grim reaper beyond the rule of the five demon kings, but once again, I didn't say anything. There was no reason to keep that detail to myself, but I didn't want to worry them until I knew more. There was a chance the grim reaper wasn't here to do her job. Maybe she was Zathrian's guest for some perfectly logical reason.

"What did this person look like?" Aukina asked, bringing me out of my spiral.

Astoria's green eyes were the first image that popped into my brain. There was something alluring about them, as if there were a thousand stories waiting to be told. I couldn't tell my friends that, so instead, I described her hair and her clothes. I finished with, "And her name is Astoria."

"Did she say why she was here?" Nyri asked.

She didn't have to. She was a grim reaper. "Just that she was looking for someone to show her around, but I wasn't exactly in the mood after dangling in the air and breaking my nails."

"Not your nails," Aukina said, no sympathy in her voice.

I narrowed my eyes, debating about giving her the same gesture I had given Reamann. I decided her offense didn't warrant a snarky comment and shifted on the grass. I should've asked Astoria questions before telling her she wasn't welcomed. Maybe then I wouldn't have been left fearing the worst.

I closed my eyes, taking in the last bit of warmth I'd get for a while. The sun made my blood boil, and I loved it. I only wished it could burn away the fear blooming in my soul.

"Just let me know if Zathrian knows anything," I said, my voice rougher than usual.

"Sure," Nyri said before settling into simple conversations about the day-to-day lives of the residents of Ethlow, as if there wasn't a deathbringer walking the grounds.

I stared at the rows of bugs on my wall, wishing they had the answer no one else did. I had collected my first pinned bug before ever arriving at Ethlow, but I had kept my collection small before. It was difficult to carry much when I traveled with my mentor, Axilya. She taught me everything I knew about healing and kept me from completely losing myself after I broke away from the coven I stayed at after first turning into a vampire.

My collection covered my walls now that I had a stable home at Ethlow. It was quiet compared to the life I had before, but I didn't mind. I hadn't hurt anyone since arriving at the estate, and I refused to let myself fall into that path again.

I thought about all the visits I had had in the past week, wondering if any of the injuries were enough to lead to death, but they all had been minor. When I hit a dead end, and the bugs didn't speak to me, I found myself wandering the estate again.

The halls were filled with ghosts, echoing the horrors that once lived in a place like Ethlow. In the rest of Kinzlea, there were rumors about the poor souls that found themselves at Ethlow, mostly from the humans who formed the cities in the territory. Humans were afraid of demons—rightfully so—which led them to say terrible things about the demon king. It was the reason I had found myself at the doorstep of Ethlow over fifty years ago.

I had nothing left, and I felt like I deserved to be punished. Only, it wasn't like that.

If the humans knew what a puppy Zathrian was, would they still call him a monster?

As I passed by the storage, I heard faint music coming from inside. I continued on, not interested in whatever party was occurring behind the door. I passed through the mess hall, the smell of cookies lingering in the air. I passed by the laundry room, sewing room, public bathing area, and every other area on the first floor. It was a path I had made nearly every night since coming to Ethlow.

I barely paid attention to my surroundings as my body moved on autopilot. It was something to distract me in the lifeless hours of the night, but it didn't stop my mind from spinning.

"Don't you get lonely wandering by yourself like that?"

I stopped, my body tense. Even when I wasn't paying attention, my instincts were good about picking up the sounds of other residents. Only it wasn't another resident. I turned slowly, anticipating the appearance of the grim reaper.

Astoria sat on top of a statue of a wyvern in the grand hall. She kicked her feet with her head tilted to the side.

"I like the quiet night." My fingers tensed at the memory of being caught in a trap.

"I don't like silence," Astoria said. She jumped off the statue, and my body lurched forward, ready to catch her from the long fall.

She disappeared before she hit the ground, appearing behind me. Her giggle rang in my ears.

"Are you a sadist?" I demanded. I tried to remind myself that my anger was wasted on the reaper. I needed to ask the questions I failed to when I first met her, which required keeping my cool.

Her eyes sparkled like an emerald. "Maybe just a bit. What can I say? I like seeing the surprise on a pretty face like yours."

I opened my mouth to argue, but I didn't know what to say. The compliment threw me off. Instead, I cleared my throat, trying to regain my focus. "Why are you here?"

"I'm taking a break. I thought maybe we could play a game." If what I said to the reaper the last time I saw her bothered her, she didn't show it.

"Why would I play a game with you? Your last game broke my nails." I flashed my cracked nails as proof. I hadn't had a chance to see the pixie who usually did my manicure since my last encounter with the reaper.

"Nails are easy to fix. I thought you would've already, but maybe you like that they remind you of me."

I gave her a flat look. "You're insane if you think I'd keep them like this because of you."

"Insane but fun." Her wink made my stomach twist.

The last thing I wanted to do was have fun with Astoria. I needed to stop letting her distract me. "You're here because someone is going to die, aren't you?"

Astoria scrunched her face. "I don't want to talk about death. I want to get to know you."

"Why?"

"Because maybe I want a friend. Is that so bad?" For a moment, a shadow flickered across her face. Despite her upbeat voice, there was something she was hiding beneath her colorful exterior.

I wanted to push her to tell me why she had come to Ethlow, but my gut told me that she wouldn't answer me unless I played her game. "And what would being your friend entail?"

Her face lit up at my question. "Tell me one of your deepest, darkest secrets, and then I'll tell you one of mine. Then our friendship will be sealed forever."

"That's not how friendship works." Friends took time to build. It wasn't about secrets and games.

"Humor me, and maybe I'll humor you with the answers you want." She knew what I wanted, but she wasn't going to give me answers easily.

I had to humor her with a proper answer, and something told me she would see through any lies. I took a shaky breath.

"I sucked the life out of a child once, and it was the worst day of my life. The worst part was that I enjoyed it." My hands shook as I spoke the secret I had never said out loud before. I waited for the hatred to flood Astoria's eyes, but it never happened. Instead, her face softened.

"If I could give up being a grim reaper to listen to an orchestra play for the rest of my life, I would," Astoria said.

I pressed my lips tight. Her secret paled in comparison to mine, but it wasn't my place to call her out. "You like music that much."

Astoria grabbed my forearms and started spinning me around the room. "Music soothes my soul. It tells a story that words couldn't possibly describe. It is freeing and just lovely." She spun me around and then dipped me without warning, making me yelp.

She smiled down at me. Her warmth surrounded me, making me feel flushed and leaving a lightness in my chest that was strange.

Astoria's eyes went cloudy, and a frown carved out her face, dropping her mood. It made me want to touch her lips to soften the hard lines. She pulled me back to my feet and let me go. "Work calls. I must go." She disappeared without a proper goodbye, and a familiar emptiness washed over me.

Chapter 3

I stretched my fingers out, looking at the three cracked nails. There was no reason to delay getting them fixed. It looked horrendous and did *not* remind me of the reaper.

Knock! Knock! Knock! I rapped my knuckles against the door that had carvings of a sun and various swirls.

Screams of young children echoed from behind the door I stood in front of. I waited, surprised to hear the calls of the youngins. Elcy was the teacher of the estate, but it was supposed to be her day off. The door swung open, and the cries and laughter of the kids echoed out. A short pixie stood in front of the door. Her blonde hair was tied in a bun—it stopped the younger ones from pulling it.

There were bags under Elcy's eyes, but her white freckles glowed in the early morning light, balancing the tiredness of her eyes.

"Satella, I'm surprised to see you." She had a human girl on her hip. At three years old, Arbella was the youngest resident of the demon king's estate. Under normal circumstances, the child wouldn't have been allowed to stay at the demon king's estate, but her older brother had begged Viridian, the master of the estate, to let her stay. I didn't understand why the demon had accepted the boy's pleas, since he believed children belonged out in the world, not locked up in a demon's estate.

I held up my hands. "I'm surprised to see the children."

"Kavra is sick today and asked me to fill in." Elcy was like that, always offering to help those in need. It made me debate about leaving, but I hated the state of my cracked nails.

"Do you have time to redo my nails? I know you're busy, so it's fine if you can't today."

"Come in." Elcy opened the door wider. Her pixie wings were tucked away. Toddlers had a tendency to grab anything they could, and pixie wings were fragile.

"Hi, Satella!" Thalanil called out. At the age of fourteen, he was one of the older children in the horde that lived at Ethlow. He was respectful and kind. His only flaw was that he was a werewolf—not that I held his genetics against him. Usually.

"Hey, Nil. Are you behaving for Miss Elcy?" I had gotten to know the children well. All of them had arrived at the demon king's estate after I had, and children were prone to accidents and colds.

"I'm always on my best behavior." Thalanil smiled sweetly. If it wasn't for his awful scent, he could have passed as human, at least until he came of age and started shifting into his wolf form.

"Right," I said, dragging out the syllable. He was at the chaotic stage of his life, and I didn't understand how the caretakers handled all the children or how Elcy taught them with their varying ages.

"Why don't you and Galia start a game of hide and seek with the others while Satella and I talk?" Elcy suggested. Most of the children were old enough that they didn't need constant supervision.

"Yes, ma'am." He saluted Elcy before running off to the others.

Elcy's face dropped. "I hate when he calls me ma'am. It makes me feel old."

"I know for a fact I'm older than you." I first arrived at Ethlow five decades ago, but that was just a fraction of my lifespan.

Elcy chuckled. "You don't know how old I am." She was right. Pixies were immortal, just like vampires. She had been at the estate for less time than me, but that didn't mean anything.

"You're young at heart. I'm an old soul."

Elcy lifted her brows, not buying my statement. "We could argue about that all day. Let's focus on fixing your nails before the children get out of hand." She handed me Arbella and settled into her nail station. It was tucked in a corner to save it from the children messing with her supplies.

I shifted the human on my hip and sat, placing my left hand on the table for Elcy to work on. Her official title was teacher of the estate, but she did nails for anyone who asked, as long as they made an appointment. She was a talented artist—not that she let anyone see her work outside of her nail art.

The pixie got to work on my nails while I distracted the toddler, so full of life. It was a shame she ended up somewhere like Ethlow. Most who showed up at the demon king's estate had faced horrors no one else should ever have to face. The stories of the children were the worst.

"So, are you going to tell me how you broke your nails?" Elcy asked as she worked. Her ears twitched as one of the children screamed. We waited for crying or any signs that something was wrong, but after a moment, giggles followed, signaling the okay.

"I went for one of my nightly walks, and I met someone."

The pixie raised her brows, but she kept working. "Someone, as in *someone*?"

"No," I snapped. "She is arrogant, and I don't think she was supposed to be at Ethlow. I got caught in her trap. It was annoying." The annoyance wasn't as strong as the first night I broke my nails. My interactions with Astoria last night had felt different.

"Are you sure it wasn't one of Malse's traps?" The pixie mixed up the next color, and made quick work of my nails. She was skilled at listening to others. I was sure others liked to talk to her about their troubles while she worked on their nails.

"No, that gnome couldn't pull something like that off. Besides, Astoria took full credit. She was proud she trapped me."

Elcy chuckled. "It sounds like you like her."

I clenched my teeth at the accusation. I focused on Arbella, bouncing her on my leg as a distraction. "I could never like someone like her."

The pixie smirked as she set her paintbrush down. She had already finished my nails. "You can't control who you fall for."

"I'm not interested in a relationship." I had tried that before, and it had become too difficult. No one understood my struggles as a vampire, even other vampires. They didn't understand the hatred that burned in my core, which always led to arguments. I was better off alone.

"So who is this person, anyway? I haven't heard of any new residents. Is she one of the king's guests?" Elcy asked.

I hadn't stopped thinking about Astoria since our last interaction. She was skilled at avoiding my questions. "I don't know, but I'm determined to find out.

Chapter 4

I waited for night to come before stepping outside my room. During the day, it was my responsibility to handle the injuries of the estate, but there were many days when I saw no one. Most days had a handful of minor injuries at most. It was rare for others to need my healing abilities at night, which gave me freedom to roam, as long as I stayed inside.

Ethlow only had two rules for the residents. *Do your assigned work. Don't go outside at night.* The first rule was to keep the estate running smoothly. The second was to keep us safe. At night, horrid creatures passed through the veil of the underworld in search of the demon king's magic. His protective barrier only extended to the walls of the estate, so anyone who stepped outside at night was subjected to horrible creatures that could kill immortals.

It was an easy rule for most to follow. The residents feared the creatures that lurked in the night.

For me, it was different. There were nights my bones itched to explore the darkness. It was as if my soul called out to the moon, eager to be reunited. Only I was sure vampires didn't have souls. That was stripped away the day two fangs pierced my neck, forever changing my life.

I stopped in the grand entrance, my gaze lingering on the thick, crimson curtains that kept the night out of the estate. I couldn't keep it from calling out to me. I felt the thrum of the shadows pulling me forward, begging me to step outside just once. A life locked inside at night and free during the day wasn't part of the design of vampires. I was a creature of the night, but I fought against my instincts, hating what I had become.

At night, when no one was around, it was harder to ignore the lack of pulse where my heart was. I walked along the marble floor, practically floating along, making no noise with each step. My fingers grazed the velvet curtains, pulling them back to reveal the white light of the moon. Shadows twisted under the light, searching for anything to devour.

I had once been like that. Moving mindlessly from one town to the next in search of something to make me feel alive. I clawed at anything that reminded me of my human life, but without a heartbeat, very few things made me feel alive.

I died too young. I had only been twenty-two at the time. My brain wasn't fully developed at the time of the change. Too young to make any serious life decisions, but it didn't matter. Turning into a vampire hadn't been a choice.

I felt the shift in the air before I heard her voice.

"Thinking about going outside?" Astoria's voice echoed in the emptiness of the grand hall.

I let the curtain fall, knowing there was nothing out there for me. "I was wondering when you'd show up."

Her footsteps were silent, but I felt her presence move closer. It was as if she had an energy that brought life into the room. "Don't you mean if?" Her voice was a whisper on the wind, barely gracing my ear.

I turned slowly. Astoria had her hands clasped behind her back, and she leaned forward, putting her face only inches from mine. Her strange power pulsed through the air, reminding me of her otherworldly nature.

I refused to step back. I didn't want her to think she had power over me.

"No." I looked her up and down. "I knew you'd find me again."

A light danced in her eyes. Game on. "A cocky little vampire, aren't you?"

I smirked, swallowing the questions burning my throat. I wanted to ask why she was here, and if she planned to take a soul, I had to know whose soul she was here for. But if I asked any of those questions, it gave her control over the situation. She made it clear she wouldn't give up those answers easily. I needed to know why there was a grim reaper at the demon king's estate, but if I knew anything about Astoria, it was that she liked to play games.

"Well, I'm off. Have a good night." I walked past the reaper, grateful I didn't have a heartbeat to give away my anxiety. I was taking a gamble. If she didn't take the bait, I could lose my one chance to discover the truth of why she was at the estate and why no one seemed to know about her visit.

"Where are you going?" She floated across the floor, not making a single sound as she followed. I was painfully aware of her presence, aware of every little movement she made.

"I have to check on my bugs." This wasn't true. I had checked on them earlier, but I wanted her to think I didn't care about her. I needed her to chase me, because I didn't chase after anyone.

"The bugs on your wall?"

Her question made my chest tighten, but I couldn't let her see that. Astoria knew more about me than she should've. She said my name before I introduced myself to her, and she knew what the inside of the infirmary looked like. Her knowledge of me was unnerving.

"No," I said. If I asked her how and why she knew all of that, she could hold the information over my head. Or she could tell me an answer I didn't want to hear. Cool and aloof. That was the mask I had to keep on my face.

"What bugs?" She floated next to me, making it clear that she wasn't going anywhere. My plan was working. She was hooked.

"Do you want to see?"

"Yes." Her eyes danced with curiosity.

My lips betrayed me, tugging into a sly smile.

No one ever wanted to see my bugs. People had misconceptions that bugs were icky and gross. They didn't see the beauty in them like I did. They had lives, just like any other living being or animal.

They were shorter with the sole intention of surviving as a species, but it only made them more beautiful. They didn't have time for lies and games.

I pushed into the infirmary, pausing to look at the collection of pinned bugs on the walls. Many didn't understand my fascination with the pinned bugs, many calling it morbid. Maybe it was morbid to hang dead things on my wall, but there was a beauty to it. Bugs were essential to nature. They worked hard, despite their shorter lifespans.

They were misunderstood by the population, something I understood deeply.

As a vampire, most saw me as a predator, unable to look past the surface. Even at Ethlow, I got strange looks, especially from newcomers. To them, I was the enemy. Their blood fueled my body. What they didn't understand was I didn't want most of their blood. I had particular tastes. Not to mention I never drained a victim, at least not after getting my urges under control.

A shiver ran down my spine, thinking about the darkness that once ruled my life.

Astoria tilted her head, but I ignored the curious gaze. I didn't feel like diving into the secret I had spilled.

I moved through my workroom, picking up my pace as I led her to my private chambers. My room was connected to the infirmary in case of emergencies. I was the only healer in the entire estate, but it wasn't an issue most days. Most injuries were minor, and residents didn't get sick often, except in the winter. Many bodies didn't handle snowfall as well as a vampire who should have thrived in the cold.

I held the door to my room open for Astoria, even though I had a feeling she could find her way into the room without an invitation, unlike me. She went straight to my bed and jumped on it. Her chest bounced as she settled onto the mattress, but I quickly tore my eyes away.

I focused on the two glass cages sitting on my desk opposite to my bed. I pulled out a box of mealworms and picked one out before opening the tank on the left. "This is Midnight, my dancing black tarantula." I dropped the worm inside and shut the tank.

Astoria leaned in. "She's pretty."

"You're not afraid of spiders?" If handled correctly, Midnight was as harmless as any other pet, but the moment someone saw more than four legs, they decided otherwise.

The grim reaper leaned back, stretching her arms high above her head as she settled on the bed. "When you've seen as much death as I have, there's not much to be afraid of."

I gripped the desk and focused on my breathing. "Is that why you're here? To cause death?"

Astoria blinked at me, no longer lying down. "Grim reapers don't cause death."

My room felt too small with the two of us in it. I didn't need more space than this on most days, but having a reaper in my room made me wish I had demanded a space separate from the healer's room, instead of insisting it was connected.

I turned to face Astoria, her lips puckered with frustration. "Why are you here, then?"

She didn't blink as she said, "I can't tell you."

"Are you here for me?" I wished I had a heartbeat. It'd give me something to focus on other than the silence in my body. My eyes focused on Midnight, watching her stalk her meal.

Astoria moved across the room, not bothering to answer my question. Instead, she looked at the tank below the window. "Tell me about who they are."

Part of me wanted to demand she answer my question, but I had already lost control of the situation. I turned back to my babies. "These are rainbow hornworms. This one here is Afternoon Tea. This is Midnight Snack. And that one in the corner is Breakfast Bagel. Aren't they cute?" Looking at my hornworms calmed my thoughts. "I want to raise them through their life cycle. Soon, they will cocoon, and a few weeks after that, they will turn into beautiful rainbow moths."

Astoria opened the cage and picked up Afternoon Tea. Her touch was gentle, but I watched her closely. If she hurt the hornworm— "And what about after they've turned into moths?"

I knew exactly what she meant. Moths had short lifespans, especially compared to the lifespan of a vampire. Death was inevitable. "When they have lived a full and happy life and succumb to death, I will get them pinned and put them on my wall to honor their memory."

The corner of Astoria's lip tugged into a phantom smile. "For someone afraid of death, you are awfully fascinated by it."

"I understand that life and death go hand in hand." It was impossible to ignore that fact. Everyone I had known in my childhood was long gone, but the world had moved on without them.

"Then why are you so afraid of it?" She set the hornworm back in its cage before giving me her full attention. Her face was soft without a single wrinkle on it. She looked close to the age I was when I stopped aging, but I knew that was as much of a lie as my own face. There was something compelling about the woman who stood in front of me. There were few around me that had lived as many lives as me, but I was sure the reaper had lived more. It made me want to hear her stories and learn what lay behind those eyes.

"I'm not afraid of death. I don't like it. There's a difference."

"There is a difference." She stepped closer, and her scent hit my nose. She smelled like the morning after a rainstorm, like a fresh start. "But you are afraid of death."

"I am immortal. There is no reason to be afraid."

"Perhaps. Or maybe there's more reason to be afraid. You may live for a long while yet, but your friends will not. You should learn to come to terms with it, because death is inevitable. For you and for your friends." She took a step back and disappeared, leaving me to process what she said. More than ever, I was convinced she was here for me or for someone else I knew.

That thought gripped my heart for the rest of the night.

Chapter 5

I stood outside the demon king's office, inspecting my nails carefully. They were in perfect condition, no traps or anything else messing them up. Days had passed without an appearance from the grim reaper, and life had continued on. That should've been a good thing, since it meant no one had died, but I hadn't gotten any answers I had been looking for.

I wasn't surprised when I was summoned to the demon king's office. It was a matter of time before Nyri told her mate about the intruder, leading Zathrian to question me further. My only surprise was how long it took for him to summon me.

The door swung open, and the demon king greeted me with a smile. There had been a time when it was forbidden to interact with the demon king. The rule had been put in place shortly before I arrived due to an incident with one of the residents. It had left the king of Kinzlea a mystery to me and many others for decades. Then a human—Nyri—showed up and changed everything. She had risked her life to meet with the demon king, and it had paid off in the end.

It was strange seeing him look like he was at peace when he had been a mysterious brooding force for my entire time at Ethlow.

Seeing him and Nyri together was stranger. He was wrapped around her finger, despite him being the most powerful demon in the kingdom and her being a human with simple magic.

I dipped my head in greeting. "Good morning, Zathrian."

"That's King Zathrian to you," Viridian corrected in the background. The demon was the king's second in command, and he played the part well. He was considered the master of the house, and he ensured the estate ran smoothly while Zathrian focused on the rest of Kinzlea. He was good at his job, but I was convinced he had a permanent stick up his ass. A good lay would fix that. The problem was finding someone who could tolerate the demon enough to spread his or her legs for him.

"Hello, Viridian." I smirked at the master of the house and watched him bristle.

"That's Master Viridian to you." His power surged in warning, but his reaction only fueled my motives. He was a stickler for the rules, which included calling others by their proper titles. I had been alive too long to care about that.

"Now, now, Viridian. There's no need for labels. We're all friends here." Zathrian opened his arms wide, and his smile glowed. He was more puppy than he was demon. If it wasn't for the horns coming out of his head, I never would've thought he was one of the most powerful demons in the realm.

"I don't have friends," Viridian said.

"I'm not surprised." I smiled when his glare intensified.

He stretched his fingers, flashing his sharp nails that could gut me with a single slash. It was impossible to take the warning seriously when I knew the master of the house was sworn to protect the residents. He would never let a little verbal disrespect push him into breaking his oath. It was a dangerous line to walk, but it was fun.

Zathrian stepped away from the door and moved to his desk. "You're probably wondering why I called you here."

I stood outside the door, waiting. "I'm assuming it's because of a conversation Nyri and I had."

Zathrian's eyes widened in surprise. "Yes, how did you know?"

I thought about sassing the demon king, but it was harder to cross that line with him. Even though he was a sweetheart who loved my friend, he was the ruler of Kinzlea. "Just a guess."

"Are you going to come inside any time soon?" Viridian asked, his voice dry.

I smiled as sweetly as I could at the demon. "As soon as I get an invitation, I will. I'm a vampire, remember?" I motioned to the invisible barrier stopping me from crossing the threshold into the demon king's office.

Viridian's eyes glowed with mischief, as if he was thinking about leaving me outside.

"Come in, come in," Zathrian said quickly.

The magic that held my feet in place released, and I entered the room. I sat in the chair across from Zathrian, ready to pretend like Viridian didn't exist. Most cowered from the master of the house, so my rebellious nature exasperated him. I liked knowing I had that power over him.

"Can I get you anything to drink or eat before we begin?" Zathrian offered.

"Thank you for being such a great host." I flicked my eyes towards Viridian to let him know he should have been nicer. He ignored the look, but I was confident it affected him the way I wanted it to. "But no. I don't need anything. I have a meal set for tomorrow."

"Yes, of course," Zathrian said. "So Nyri told me that you met someone new in the estate?"

I nodded once. I already knew the answer to my question, but I asked it anyway. "I was wondering if there was a new resident at Ethlow." Astoria wasn't a resident. There was no reason for a grim reaper to stay at the demon king's estate, but on the slight chance I was wrong, I had to ask.

"Nyri is the latest resident to arrive," Zathrian answered, as I had expected. Not many people showed up at the demon king's estate because of the very nature of demons and the rumors that surrounded the king.

"And there are no current visitors?" I wasn't as sure about this answer. Astoria had said she was above the demon kings' rule, but that didn't mean Zathrian wasn't aware of her presence.

Viridian arched his eyebrow. "What makes you think you're privy to that information?"

I arched my eyebrow in return, matching his energy. I stood prepared to walk away. "My apologies for wasting your time." I turned, hoping my calculation worked in my favor. If they didn't know about Astoria's presence, then I had valuable information for them.

"There are no guests currently residing at the estate," Viridian said through clenched teeth. I was shocked he was the one who answered. I had expected Zathrian to break first, if not for his personality, then for the woman he had fallen in love with.

"Interesting." I turned slowly, but I didn't sit again. "Perhaps I was imagining the woman I ran into a few nights ago."

Zathrian's forehead wrinkled. "If you know anything, Satella, please tell us. If there is a chance the estate is in danger, then we need to know. There are wards around the estate that should have warned us about any intruders, and if they are failing..." He swallowed hard, genuine fear filling his eyes.

Nyri had been attacked once because of her ties to the demon king. He was afraid it would happen again. He didn't have to say any of that for me to read his face. He loved Nyri, which was dangerous in and of itself. Demons and humans weren't meant to mix. A human with a demon king was asking for trouble.

Trouble was what I was afraid of, but I wasn't sure if the powerful demons in front of me could stop whatever was already in motion.

"She said her name is Astoria, and she's a grim reaper. I didn't tell Nyri that last part, because I didn't want to worry her unnecessarily."

The air stilled. Viridian didn't move, and his irritation from before was gone, replaced by something I couldn't pinpoint.

"Good," Zathrian said. His magic stroked the air, searching for answers in the unspoken words. "It's best if you don't tell anyone else about this. The last thing we need is a panic."

That wasn't the answer I wanted. "She's here to collect a soul, isn't she?"

"Most likely," Viridian answered. "If anyone else knew about this, they would become irrational, and death would touch more lives than the one she is here for."

I swallowed my own fear. Death and I towed a fine line. If anyone could handle the knowledge of a grim reaper walking on the premises, it was me. "There's nothing you can do to stop her?"

"She is above the laws of the demon rulers," Zathrian said. "No order I gave her would affect her. It is best to let her do what she came here to do."

"Which means *you* should stay away from her," Viridian said. "It'll only get you in trouble."

Viridian was right, and the smart thing to do was stop looking for the grim reaper and keep my distance. However, it wasn't a coincidence that she appeared to me and no one else. That knowledge weighed heavily on me, and I couldn't shake the feeling that it was fate I walked into her trap.

I wasn't going to walk away from this, not until I made sure she wasn't here for one of my friends. I didn't care if she was doing her job. I wouldn't let her take someone I cared about without a fight.

Chapter 6

A knock on the door pulled me out of my stupor. I checked the clock, realizing the day had gotten away from me. Today was a slow day in the infirmary. Other than a sewing accident in the morning, I had been alone, lost in thought. I completely forgot about my appointment.

I opened the door and took in the fae warrior in front of me. Iolas stood tall, prepared to take on the precious act of giving his blood to me. His blond hair was perfectly styled, and he smelled clean. It was a requirement when I accepted blood from anyone, but especially for a warrior who spent his time sweating and training. He had learned his lesson the first time I kicked him out when he showed up drenched in sweat.

"You're looking handsome today," I said, flashing him a smile. I found the nicer I was to those who donated blood to me, the more willing they were to come back, especially when they were of the male species. And I needed them to come back.

When I first arrived at Ethlow, Viridian had told me that if I took blood from an unwilling victim, I would have been kicked out immediately. It was an easy term to agree to, since it was against my own morals to take from the unwilling. Not that the willing were difficult to find. I found males the easiest to manipulate. Painted red lips went a long way with males, especially when they thought about them pressing against their necks.

"And you're looking as beautiful as ever." He lifted my hand and kissed the back of it.

I held in my cringe. I didn't want him to know how much his touch repulsed me. "Let's go." I interlaced my fingers with his and guided him to my room. I didn't let many people in my private space, but I found it easier to take my time feeding when there was an extra door separating me from the rest of the estate. One resident walking in and screaming when she saw my fangs plunged into a neck was all it took for me to shift the location I took my meals.

There were worst residents with dark pasts at the estate. Some had committed more murders than me, but they kept to themselves and didn't look dangerous. Yet I was the one considered a fiend. As soon as someone learned I was a vampire, they liked to keep their distance. Until they needed me.

I let go of Iolas' hand and checked my makeup in the mirror as he stripped off his shirt. Things had a tendency to get... messy, and I didn't like to give more work to those who took care of laundry at the estate. Blood was particularly difficult to get out of clothing.

I looked at Iolas through the mirror, watching as he revealed his muscular torso. He was part of the guardsmen of the estate, so it was his responsibility to keep the residents safe from any attackers. Ethlow was usually at peace, but the occasional creature from the underworld broke through the shadows of the night.

The guardsmen kept those creatures from coming too close to the main building, which required intensive training that sculpted their muscles into masterpieces.

Only once Iolas was stripped from the waist up did I turn around. He was a gorgeous specimen. "Sit." I motioned to the chair in the corner of the room, not wanting to get my bed messy. I never slept in it, but there were many nights I spent wrapped in blankets—especially in the dead of winter. My bed was a sacred place, and Iolas would never find himself in it.

The fae followed my command without question. I could ask him to steal the world for me, and he wouldn't blink an eye, but he was nothing more than a means to an end.

I grabbed his thick thighs, letting myself admire the layers of muscles beneath my fingers for a moment before pushing his legs together. I crawled into his lap and straddled him. As I settled, a different hardness pressed against me. I shifted slightly, testing the friction. It had been too long since I had tangled with someone else, and the need was burning especially bright today.

I had slept with plenty of men throughout my lifetime. They were a fun time, but they had always been temporary. Most wanted more than I was able to give them.

Women were a different story. They were beautiful, soft, and smelled incredible. Their blood was something different, but I didn't have many female donors at the estate. Most were intimidated by my fangs, while men were easily swayed. But on the rare occasion I received the opportunity to indulge in the carnal pleasures of a woman... It was better than any high.

Heat crawled up my neck as my thoughts twisted to places I tried to avoid. Celibacy was better for me. It meant there was no one to see the darkness permanently staining my heart.

I extended my fangs, unable to hold back any longer. "Ready?"

"Yes," Iolas breathed. His heart slammed against his ribs beneath my fingers.

I took my time running my nails over his chest and up his neck. I didn't usually take my time with him. I liked to treat him like a quick meal before going back to work. But not tonight.

His pulse thrummed against the pads of my fingers as I traced his veins. His body was warm beneath me, something I missed about my own body. I missed the pulse of my heart in moments of fear and excitement. I missed feeling alive. The day my life had been stolen away from me was the day I became the walking dead.

But just for a moment, I could borrow Iolas' life. I could use his heart to remember what it felt like to have my own.

My fangs scraped against his skin, and the fae hissed. He was helpless beneath me, lost in the touch of a woman's body. I smelled his fear as he shifted, unable to hide the stiffness in his pants. His fear was always the strongest right before I started, but I knew how to make it go away.

I bit down, and my fangs pierced his skin as if it was butter. His blood flowed from his veins, and I let it dribble down his neck before pressing my lips against the open wounds. His blood hit my tongue, and his immortality tasted delicious. Humans tasted fine, but the older they got, the more sour their blood was, as if it was on the verge of spoiling. Faes always tasted fresh, even as the centuries passed by. It was why they were my favorite meal.

Iolas panted as I sucked on his skin. His warmth flowed down my throat, filling my body with his vitality. I ran my tongue over the wound to make sure I didn't take too much too quickly. I wanted to savor the moment. I wanted to relish in the heat that filled my body, knowing that the moment he walked away, I would feel empty and cold.

I shifted my hips, accidentally piercing my nails into his chest and making the scent of blood stronger. The noise that escaped his lips was guttural, balancing between pain and pleasure. It would've been easy to take him to bed. Once I had my fangs in someone, it was easy to influence them.

But I didn't want it that way. I didn't want someone only to scratch the itch I couldn't fully scratch on my own.

"Don't stop," Iolas whined. His eyes fluttered shut, and he placed his hand on my leg. He traced small circles on my inner thigh, slowly moving higher, testing to see if I'd stop him.

Maybe it wouldn't have been so bad to give into my desires for once. Iolas knew exactly what this was. He knew it'd never mean anything more. He was hard before I touched him. If I was going to give in to my needs, he would be the one to do it with. He was handsome, and he was under my spell.

I didn't stop him as he slid his hand higher and higher. I sucked on his neck harder, getting carried away. I closed my eyes, as he rubbed between my legs over my pants.

Yes, it'd feel nice to let myself enjoy the muscular body of the male for a moment. He pressed harder, and a soft moan escaped my lips.

I imagined him slipping his hands past the thin material separating us, and then—

Green eyes filled my head as I imagined her soft lips against mine. Her fingers were long, and they looked like they'd be dexterous. I was sure they'd be soft compared to the calloused fingers of the fae beneath me. I grinded against Iolas' hand, but it wasn't him I was imagining.

I ripped my mouth away from him, suddenly coming to my senses. What was I doing imagining *her* while it was Iolas who touched me?

I licked the puncture wounds, so my saliva helped slow the bleeding. Then I made him press his hand against his neck to slow the bleeding. He was paler than usual, and I knew I had gone too far.

"Don't move," I ordered, pushing down the panic bubbling up. It was a healer's job to stay calm at all times.

I grabbed gauze and a salve from the infirmary before rushing back to him. I was full of energy, unlike the fae who was missing more of his blood than usual. I scooped the milky salve onto his skin to help his body clot. Then I taped the gauze onto his neck, watching to make sure the blood didn't seep through too quickly.

He gave me a lazy smile, hovering in bliss. He didn't realize that a little longer could've resulted in serious damage. I was grateful he was fae. His magic would help him recover faster than a mortal. It didn't completely stop the guilt from creeping up.

"Stay here as long as you need to, and don't move too quickly. Don't go back to your shift today either, healer's orders."

"Viridian will be mad if I shirk my responsibilities." His eyes were half-lidded. His body was exhausted, so he wasn't going anywhere anytime soon.

"If he gives you a hard time, send him my way," I said. I wiped the lingering blood off my lips. I took a steadying breath, knowing that could have ended badly.

Chapter 7

When Iolas tried to leave, he swayed as he walked. I thought about leaving him to find his room on his own. But the thought of him collapsing in the hallway stopped me from sending him away. It was my fault he was woozy, so I put him in my bed and slipped into the infirmary. With some rest, he'd be fine. I shut the door to my private quarters and slumped against it.

As much as I hated having the fae in my bed, it was my own fault.

I had nearly lost control. The last time that happened... I swallowed hard. There was no reason to lose control, except I couldn't stop thinking about Astoria. She was here to collect someone's soul, which meant death was close. Death rarely happened within the walls of Ethlow. Despite rumors saying otherwise, the demon king's estate was one of the safest places in Kinzlea.

Between Zathrian, Viridian, and the well-trained guards, the residents were protected, unlike in the real world. In the cities belonging to Kinzlea, chaos ruled. There was little protection against animal attacks, disease, and the dark hearts of those who liked to take advantage of others. Zathrian did what he could to help his kingdom, but there was only so much he could do.

I pressed my hand where my heartbeat once was. I had been the victim of one of those dark hearts, and in return, many had been the victim of mine. I rubbed my chest, wishing for my heartbeat to return. I didn't want my immortality any longer. I didn't want to suffer through any more deaths. If Astoria was here for me, maybe I was ready.

My chest burned, and I soaked in the pain of my raw skin from rubbing too hard. Nothing I could do would ever turn back time. There was no cure for vampirism—not one I had been able to find in my time as a healer. Once injected with a vampire's venom, it infected every cell, changing a being into something unrecognizable.

I was unrecognizable.

I was a monster.

I was a bringer of death, which was why I swore to heal as many as I could. I could never atone for my sins. No matter how many lives I saved, it wouldn't bring back the lives I had taken.

Time turned into a blur as I sat there, stuck in my own guilt. No one else came to the infirmary, making it easy to slip into my thoughts and lose track of reality. Distant memories mixed with fears, turning my mind into a playground for nightmares. I needed to pull myself out of it, but I was stuck, running away from my own darkness. It was always a step behind me, a single misstep away from taking everything from me.

A light knock stopped the spinning—only it wasn't a knock on the door. It was a knock on my skull. I cracked my eyes open and was met with two glowing green eyes. For a moment, I didn't know if I was imagining it or not.

"Are you okay?" Astoria's voice was like a song, pulling me out of a sea of darkness.

I looked around the room, trying to orient myself. Hours of sitting on the floor left my body stiff. "I'm fine." I rolled my neck, trying to bring my body back to its lithe state. It didn't take much for energy to fill my muscles. Iolas blood flowed through my system, and it would fuel my body for the next several days.

Astoria was crouched, studying me closely. After a moment, she reached forward and brushed her thumb against my lower lip. I went deathly still as my lip tingled from where she touched me.

"There's blood crusted on your lip." She stood up and turned away from me. "And there's a boy in your bed." Her eyes scanned the wall of bugs. There were ninety-seven frames on the wall, so it was easy to get lost in them.

I pushed myself off the ground, ignoring the groan in my knees. Despite having immortality, my joints ached, especially in the cold. It was why I loved the sun and the heat, despite every other part of my physiology saying otherwise.

"It was feeding day," I said, a twinge of guilt shocking my chest. I had never let Iolas stay in my bed before, and I had never planned on it. That was my sacred place, but after draining too much of his blood, I owed him that much.

"Do you normally take your meals to bed?" She asked as if it was a casual question, but it felt like an accusation.

My temper flared. What I did was none of her business. "And if I do?"

Astoria shrugged. "It's no matter to me how you live your life." Her eyes moved over the frames, studying each individual specimen in the room as if they were the most interesting thing in the world.

What she thought of me didn't matter, but I found myself needing her to understand that wasn't the case. I moved in front of her, blocking her view. I wanted her to look at me as I spoke.

"I do not take my donors to bed anymore. Iolas was woozy afterwards, and I didn't want him to leave in that state. Nothing happened." I didn't know if that was a lie. I didn't sleep with the male, but to say nothing happened felt like a lie. I didn't know Astoria, though. I didn't owe her the details of my life.

She hummed, and I wasn't sure she believed me. She turned away from me to look at the other wall.

I grabbed her hand, frustrated by her response. "I didn't sleep with him."

Her eyes flicked to where I grabbed her hand. A fire danced in her eyes when they met mine again. "If you say so."

I flared my nose. "Why don't you believe me?"

"Why do you care?"

"I don't."

"Then it doesn't matter if I believe you or not, does it?" In theory, she was right. There was no reason to care what she thought happened with Iolas. I didn't know her, and she would disappear soon—as soon as she collected the soul of whoever she was here for.

The darkness slipped back into my brain, threatening to invade it like a worm. I cleared my throat and put distance between us. "You're right. It doesn't matter."

Astoria tilted her head, and it felt like she was staring straight into my soul. For all I knew, she could read a person's soul. I didn't know much about grim reapers, other than they were considered deathbringers.

The reaper grabbed my hand. Her touch was surprisingly warm. "Come on." She pulled me out of my room, not bothering to ask if I wanted to go with her.

"Where are we going?" I glanced back at the infirmary, hoping Iolas didn't wake while I was gone. I didn't want him touching any of my stuff when I wasn't there to monitor him.

"It's my time to surprise you." She moved through the estate as if she was familiar with it. She had likely been here dozens of times over the span of her time being a reaper. Unless she was new to the position.

It was shocking to realize how little I knew about Astoria and grim reapers. I had never bothered to research them. I did research on all the beings living at the estate, since it was my responsibility to keep them healthy, but in my lifetime, I hadn't run into a reaper. Before Astoria, they were a concept I hadn't thought much about.

Astoria turned and pulled me up the stairs with golden railing. The gold indicated this was the wing of the estate that belonged to the demon king. It was off limits to residents, unless they were requested.

"We aren't allowed here." I didn't fight her pull.

"Are you a rule follower?"

"Rules are there for a reason." Rules kept people safe.

"I think it's time you learn to have a little fun." We made it to the top of the stairs, but she didn't slow down. She turned and went up another flight and then another after that. We went up a total of five sets of stairs before we reached the top.

The top of the stairs led to a small room with no lighting or windows. There was only a single door. Astoria reached for the door and swung it open without a second thought. A cool breeze flooded the room, smelling of amber and moonlight. The grim reaper stepped forward, but I stepped back, pulling my hand free.

"What are you doing?"

Astoria stepped outside and twirled, making her skirt fly into the air. The door led to a terrace that overlooked the rest of the estate. A wall that came up to my belly blocked off the flat landing from the edge.

"I'm enjoying the call of the night. Aren't you going to join me?" The moonlight illuminated the reaper's skin, making it glow with ethereal beauty. Her hair bounced in waves of joy as she spun with open arms, looking freer than I had ever felt.

The call of the night pulsed in my veins, begging me to join her. "It's against the rules to leave the estate at night."

Astoria slowed her spin. "So what? Do you want to spend your life wandering the halls of this estate? You're a vampire, a creature of the night, yet you spend your nights floating aimlessly through empty halls, ignoring the call of the moon."

"I prefer the sun," I said, even as the moon begged me to step outside and bask in its glorious light. When was the last time I soaked in the night, instead of looking at it through a window?

"Lie to me all you want, but there will be a day when you need to stop lying to yourself."

I didn't know how to respond to her. I wasn't lying about anything. I preferred the sun and the warmth it provided. I liked the quietness of the estate, and I didn't miss wandering through random towns under the guise of shadows, looking for my next meal. Life at Ethlow was easy and comfortable, and it gave me time to research and raise my bugs.

"It's dangerous to leave the estate at night."

"I haven't left the estate. This is part of the building, is it not?" She walked towards the edge where a short wall separated the terrace from the fall below. In the fifty-three years I had been at Ethlow, no one had talked about access to the roof.

My feet itched to move forward, to feel the night surrounding me with nothing in its way. Maybe Astoria was right. Maybe stepping onto a terrace was different than leaving through the front door.

I almost joined the grim reaper, but then I thought about Aukina. She had nearly died from breaking the rules, and I had scolded her for it. If I joined Astoria outside, I'd be a hypocrite.

"I see you are a rule follower," Astoria said, as if she could read my decision on my face. "Shame. I thought we could have some fun." She pulled herself onto the ledge, balancing between a five-story fall and the safety of the ground.

"What are you doing? Get down from there."

Astoria spun on one foot, moving like a dancer who had spent her entire life shaping her body to move like water. When she stopped, she kept her foot hovering over the edge away from me. "As you wish." She stepped off the ledge and plunged into the darkness.

Chapter 8

I rushed to the wall, using my vampire speed to get there in a split second. I reached for Astoria's hand, but she wasn't there. My nails dug into the bricks, panic flooding my system.

A cackle exploded behind me. I whipped around and found Astoria hunched over, grabbing her stomach. "I can't believe you actually fell for that." She wiped tears from her eyes, unable to control her laughter.

"It's not funny!" I snapped. "I thought you were going to get hurt."

Astoria straightened, finally gaining control over her body. "You should've known better. You've seen me teleport before. Even if I had fallen, life and death do not affect me the same. That fall wouldn't have left a scratch on me."

I clenched my fingers into fists, digging my nails into my skin. Blood dribbled from the shallow wounds, but I didn't care, knowing it'd heal quickly. As long as I was well-fed, my body didn't need medicines and salves to heal. "I didn't have time to think. I saw you fall and reacted."

Astoria leaned forward and poked my nose. "Exactly. You stopped thinking so much, and look where you are. Outside, under the moonlight."

The moon shone on my colorless skin. The blood in my body thrummed, as if the moon was tugging on it. I spread my fingers and focused on the night that hugged me, welcoming me home. My fangs extended, just as eager as every part of me. I had forgotten what it was like to feel this way, to give into my vampiric nature and thrive in the environment woven through the cosmos for me.

I should've returned to the estate. I was outside, breaking the second rule of Ethlow, but it felt like a gray area. Zathrian's magic coated the floor, repelling the monsters of the underworld and keeping danger away from this alcove. For a moment, I felt free. The future didn't feel grim, but it was an illusion.

Astoria watched me, unblinking. Her lips curled into a soft smile. She won tonight. She got her way, and there was no point in fighting it.

But why did she bother? If she was here to collect a soul, why waste time with me at all?

The questions burned in my core, but as I stared at the moon reflecting in her eyes, I didn't want to ask them. I didn't want to ruin the moment with whys and hows, especially if what Viridian said was right. Asking those questions could cause issues.

I leaned against the wall, looking at the world around it. Nothing but trees and nature stretched on for as far as I could see. No town dared to build near the demon king's estate. The common people lived in fear of demons, even more so than vampires.

Demons had taken advantage of the common people for centuries. Their magic was heavily based in making deals, and they were known to twist terms to rule in their favor.

Not all demons were like that. The ones who ended up at Ethlow were different. They were born as demons, but that didn't define them. It didn't make them inherently evil. All it meant was they were from the underworld—just like vampires. And grim reapers.

"How long have you been a grim reaper?" I asked.

Astoria moved next to me, her forearm brushing against mine as she leaned her weight against the wall. "I've lost track. At least a millennium, I think. Maybe two. Time loses its meaning at a certain point. The day-to-day blurs together when you perform the same job day in and day out."

My life had become like that. During the day, I treated patients. At night, I wandered the hallways. There were weeks when I couldn't remember how long ago I arrived at Ethlow. My friends grounded me. They broke up the monotony of the days, but it didn't stop the years from blending together.

"How do you do it? How do you handle seeing so many deaths?"

Astoria looked to the sky. There was no pain nor happiness in her expression. It was as if she had slipped a mask off, or maybe she put one on. "Death is a part of life, necessary for the growth of the world. I am there to take a soul to the other side. I become what they need in their darkest moment. I help them find peace when no one else can."

I brushed my pinky against Astoria's, and it made me want to move closer. I wanted to lean into her heat, borrowing it for only a moment, but I stopped myself. She wasn't mine to borrow. "Sounds like a difficult and lonely life."

"It can be," she admitted. "But I find ways to keep myself entertained."

"Like trapping vampires in nets?" My lips betrayed me, pulling into a small smile. I wanted to stay mad at her for ruining my nails, but under the moonlight, I couldn't bring myself to feel angry.

"That and other things." She tapped her pinky against mine and smiled. I bit my bottom lip, a giddiness creeping through my veins.

I wanted to ask what other things in hopes I was the other things, but the fear of rejection stopped the words from forming. "So what's next?"

Her warmth disappeared before she appeared on the wall again. "Next, you join me up here." She walked along the top of the wall, balancing with ease. She glanced over her shoulder, waiting for me to join her.

There was a time I lived my life without a care. I didn't worry about following rules. I didn't know when that had changed. I pressed my palms into the brick, the heat of the day still lingering. With a small hop, my feet landed on top of the wall. Astoria offered her hand to me, appearing directly next to me.

She pulled me up. Despite her slender figure and soft skin, she was strong. My legs wobbled as I looked over the edge at the black roofs covering the different levels of the estate, but Astoria held firmly, keeping me steady.

I took a step, testing my balance. There was a time my core held me firm, and I could run along walls in the middle of the night without an issue, but decades of complacency made those skills wither. Vampires had a natural physicality that many mortals lacked, but without proper training, even those talents faded. Astoria followed me, holding my hand the entire time.

Each step I took revived muscles that had long slumbered. As I reached the corner of the wall, I let go of the reaper and moved on my own. My torso wobbled a few times, but I regained my balance. As my confidence grew, so did my stride.

After completing a circle of the area, I stopped. My body hadn't felt that light in decades. I stopped and inhaled the night air, taking in the buzz beneath my skin. It was as if a taste of the night wasn't enough. My body begged me to disappear into the shadows created by the trees. The darkness called to me, knowing I belonged to it, not the world I had found myself in. I was a creature of night and dark, but I had been fighting it for as long as I could remember.

Emotions welled in my chest, and tears quickly followed. I felt free, but that only reminded me of how trapped I felt. My life would have been completely different if my mortality hadn't been stolen away from me. For the longest time, I had thought it would've been better. I wouldn't have been tied to the life force of others, constantly worried I'd take it too far and kill again.

But I'd also be dead.

Astoria stood next to me, not saying anything. There was nothing for her to say. She could never understand the life I mourned and the life I had come to love. I loved my friends and my bugs. I loved healing others and soothing their pain. Yet, I had been lost in the darkness, suppressing my carnal desires. I was still living in that darkness, but now it felt as if there was a beam of light breaking through the shadows.

There was no reason a rooftop and a grim reaper should've changed anything.

I wiped my cheeks with the back of my hands, careful not to mess up the color on my eyes.

"When's the last time you stepped outside at night?" Astoria's presence was a warm breeze. It was as if she was all over my skin, even though there was a step between us. But with her there, I didn't feel alone.

"I don't remember. Before I came to Ethlow." I understood the need for the rules, especially with more fragile beings living in the estate. The demon king took them in, making him responsible for their lives, and the creatures that lurked in the shadows could harm some of the strongest immortals. Even on the roof, I felt the evil lurking in the shadows below, calling out for me to join them.

They'd likely kill me if I did, but I was just a different branch on the same tree. The blood that ran through my veins was an agglomeration of other's lives. My own blood had long faded.

"You are a creature of the night. There's no sense in denying it," Astoria said. "The longer you fight who you are, the more time you'll waste."

It wasn't that easy. At Ethlow, I wasn't chased out of towns and cities for who I was. I could've found a vampire coven to stay with, but the one I had stayed with for a while lived a life without regard to mortals. It wasn't a life I wanted.

"I have all the time to waste, because I'm immortal." I had heard many complain about wanting to live forever, but they never understood it wasn't as easy as they thought. Watching the world crumbling while I moved on wasn't easy. Why did I get to live forever when there were others with pure souls that died young? "Besides, it's not like my life matters in this world. Even if I died tomorrow, it would continue on without me."

Astoria turned towards me, the movement compelling me to face her. "Death is not easy, and your life matters more than you think."

"If you knew the things I have done, you wouldn't be saying that." When I closed my eyes, I remembered the faces of the lives I took when I was drunk on blood and power. The faces that haunted me the most were the children.

"You matter to your friends, and you matter to this world. You can change the fate of so many lives with the gift you've been given."

More tears fell. "I was cursed, not given a gift."

Astoria pressed her hand over where my heart lay dormant. "I am not talking about you being a vampire. I'm talking about your heart. The way you care for others will lead you down a road that will change more than you could ever imagine."

I wanted to believe her. I wanted to believe in a world where I did more good than harm, but after what nearly happened with Iolas, it was difficult to imagine. "Why did you come to Ethlow?"

I had been putting off asking that, knowing it'd lead to something I didn't want to face. "Are you here for me?"

The smile she gave drooped with grief. "I cannot tell you."

I stepped towards her, nearly losing balance as my anger affected my balance. She grabbed me, steadying my body, but I didn't want her to touch me. "You're a grim reaper. You are here because someone is going to die. I need to know if it's me or one of my friends."

Astoria held my gaze, her eyes burning with an intensity that shook my core. "Death is inevitable. You need to learn to accept that now, before it tears you apart."

Before I could ask a question, a caw echoed around us. A shadow danced through the moonlight, moving towards us. Astoria lifted her arm, and a crow landed on it.

"If you're here to collect one of my friends, I'm not going to stand by and watch it happen." My chest tightened, making it difficult to breathe.

Astoria let go of me and ran her finger under the crow's beak. "I'm surprised to see you, Kestria. Isn't it dangerous for you to be here?"

Caw! Caw! The bird's call almost sounded like *Mind your business,* but I knew I was imagining it. Crows didn't speak common.

"Don't ignore me," I said, needing Astoria to tell me why she was here. As a healer, it was my responsibility to save the lives of Ethlow. If there was anything I could do to stop her from collecting one of the lives at the demon estate, I had to do something about it.

"You should go back inside," Astoria said. Her face and voice were tight, as if something was wrong. "A certain demon needs you."

The crow flew off, and Astoria disappeared, leaving me on the rooftop alone.

Chapter 9

My head spun as I took my time heading back to the infirmary. One moment, Astoria had reminded me what it felt like to be free. The next, I wanted to shake her until she told me why she was at Ethlow.

It was a lot for one night, which made me want to lay in bed and close my eyes to decompress.

Except my bed wasn't empty. Knowing the fae was in my private space made my head pound. I rubbed my temples, regret setting in. I should've kicked him out, even if he was disoriented.

Only that wasn't something I could do as a healer. I made a promise to myself to help whoever I could—especially those I had caused harm to.

My feet dragged through the hallways, the burst of energy from before completely gone. Once I made it back to the infirmary, I stumbled into the patient's bed and closed my eyes. I didn't want to think for a moment.

The door burst open a second later, and I flew off the bed at the sudden intrusion. Two large and looming figures stood in the doorway, and the scent of blood stung my nose, making my mouth water. The figure on the left was unfamiliar to me. He was as tall as the demon king, his muscles threatening to burst through his blood-soaked shirt. The energy that flowed off of him was powerful and almost suffocating. Whoever he was, he was a fearsome demon, but he wasn't important, not as Viridian was slung over his shoulder.

The blood belonged solely to the master of the house, from what I could tell. Viridian's teal hair was plastered to his face with sweat and dirt. His usually clean butler's outfit was ripped and torn in several locations, revealing deep cuts in his skin. His eyes were half lidded, and he was struggling to stay conscious.

A surge of energy filled my body as my emergency mode kicked in. "Set him on the bed," I said to the stranger.

The dark-haired demon dragged Viridian onto the cot. I grabbed clean gauze and rushed to Viridian. I had never seen the master of the house in anything but perfect condition, so it was strange to see him half-unconscious, dark purple blood pouring out of him. The largest wound was in his chest, but there was too much blood to identify how he was injured.

"What happened?" I needed to know if there were magical aspects I was dealing with, because that changed my course of treatment.

"You are not privileged with that information," the other demon responded.

I pressed the gauze in Viridian's chest to slow the bleeding. "If you want me to save him, then you will tell me what happened."

"You will help him, or it will be your life." His deep voice was firm and unwavering. It was clear he had no intention of giving me specifics.

"If he dies, it'll be on you, not me."

I grabbed more gauze, discarding the soiled ones. The bleeding wasn't slowing, so I needed to find a way to close the injury. My mind whirled, unable to believe who was beneath my hands. Viridian was a powerful demon. He should have been able to heal himself, which meant whatever or whoever attacked him had to use something that dulled his magic.

"Give me that tray," I said. If Viridian didn't have magic, his body would have to be treated as if he was mortal. Most mortals wouldn't survive the amount of blood loss or a large hole in their chest.

"I'm not your assistant. I am King Jathral." One of the five demon kings of the realm. His presence at Ethlow only raised more questions I didn't have time to ask.

"You mean the fuckhole who nearly killed my friend?" I bared my fangs, rage distracting me from my patient. I had heard plenty about the king of Mithcourt and knew I hated him.

"I had no intention of killing her," he said. He didn't move, ignoring my instructions. It was as if he didn't care if Viridian lived or died. "She and Zathrian needed a good scare."

I wanted to kill him, and if it weren't for Viridian bleeding out on my table, I might have attacked him. It was my job to put aside my personal qualms to care for patients. "Grab me that tray. Now." A pulse of silence flowed between us, neither of us moving. I wasn't going to back down from the arrogant bastard standing in my room, seemingly unhurt.

The muscle in his jaw feathered. He didn't say anything, but he grabbed the tray, handing it to me. I shifted over and gestured to Viridian with my chin.

"If you are going to be here while I do this, then you will help." I ignored the flare of magic that caressed my skin. The demon in the room with me could kill me with ease. My vampiric strength couldn't stop an attack from someone like him, but I didn't care. "And don't argue with me. A part of you cares that he lives, so you will listen to me."

"Fine," he growled. "But if you ever think about bossing me around again—"

"I don't care who you are or what title you hold." I interrupted, not interested in listening to an arrogant demon waving around his dick. "Apply pressure."

He grunted, but he didn't argue, taking over the pressure on the wound. I grabbed the scissors from the tray and cut Viridian's shirt. I needed a clear field if I was going to save his life. His torso was a map of the battle that had taken place. Slices covered his arms. The battle had begun with taunting moves. Whoever attacked him wanted to show him he was too slow to stop the attacker. First the arms—they had begun to seal. Then his thighs. Those cuts leaked blood, tainting his pants with dark purple blood. The worst wound was in his chest, but I struggled to read the story there. Some sort of weapon was slammed into him, barely missing his heart. It had started out as a clean wound, but then it had been twisted, ripping the skin.

It was a gruesome battle from a skilled attacker—I'd have to digest that later.

I grabbed a bottle of clear liquid to clean out the wound to prevent infections. Demons didn't deal with normal disease and infection, but without knowing what had happened, I wasn't about to take any chances.

"When I count to three, move the dressing," I ordered. "One. Two. Three."

Jathral removed the gauze, and I poured the antiseptic over Viridian's wound. He screamed, lurching forward and baring his sharp canines.

"Hold him down!"

Jathral grabbed Viridian's shoulders and pinned him to the bed, while I grabbed his thighs, fighting against his firm muscles to stop him from tearing the wound further. He couldn't afford more blood loss. My muscles strained against the demon, but I refused to back down.

Viridian slumped against the bed, his eyes fluttering shut. His chest heaved up as his body fought against the injuries.

The wound on his chest was wide and deep. I needed to close it to stop him from bleeding out.

Could demons even bleed out?

My brain searched through all the texts I had read during my time at Ethlow. Many demons had healing abilities, but some lesser demons couldn't heal themselves.

Regular weapons could harm lower demons, but stronger demons were often unaffected by regular metal, even iron.

Powerful demons could only be killed by magic or poison.

Seraphims were the direct enemy of demons. Their magic was lethal to demons in high quantity—their fire able to burn the soul of the demon.

"What are you doing?" Jathral snapped.

"Tell me what happened." I stared the demon down.

"I cannot tell you."

"Even if it means his life?"

"Yes." His eyes were cold, and his lips were a fortress. I wasn't going to get the answers I needed that could save Viridian's life.

"Can you heal him?" The ability to heal others was a rare gift, even among powerful demons.

Jathral's crooked smile made my stomach churn. "If you make a deal with me, I can lend you my power to heal him yourself."

"I'm not making a deal with you." Deals with demons were dangerous, especially with ones like Jathral who saw mortals as beneath him. I would have to use traditional methods to save the master of the house.

I pushed the demon king with my shoulder, moving to my cabinet filled with my powders and potions meant to assist with healing mortals. I grabbed several bottles, not sure if any of them would help. I smeared a salve on the wound to help the blood coagulate.

I grabbed a needle and thread to start to close the wound, but when I tried to stab the skin, the needle didn't pierce it. It was as if Viridian's skin was made of rubber.

"Use this." Jathral held a thin, black needle in his hand.

I snatched it without question, knowing I couldn't waste time. The metal was cool to the touch, and it gave off a strange power I had never come across before.

"If I asked you what this is, would you tell me?" I threaded the needle with thin wire.

"No."

Just as I thought. I was the healer. I wasn't privy to secret information.

I pierced Viridian's skin, the needle moving through it with ease. With my deft hands, it only took a few moments to close the gaping wound.

"Help me flip him," I ordered. If there wasn't a demon on my table, I could've flipped him with ease, but it was as if his body was made out of osmium. Even with my vampiric strength, he felt heavy.

I didn't miss the glare from the demon king, but I ignored it. Together we rolled Viridian on his side, giving me access to his back where more blood and a gaping wound awaited my work. We went through the same process, disinfecting it, holding him down through the pain, putting on the salve before I finally stitched him up. I wrapped his torso in gauze to cover the worst wound, ignoring the firm muscles my fingers brushed over.

Once I was sure the wound on his chest wouldn't bleed out, I moved on to the smaller, less threatening cuts. Jathral watched my every move, barely giving me space to breathe. I couldn't think about the demon king of Mithcourt or why he was at Ethlow, not when there was work to be done.

After the last stitch was made, I mixed a drink with various antidotes, including charcoal, the crushed up petals of a crux flower, and shavings from a mushroom tree. Hot water mixed the ingredients together, opening up the full potential of each of the various antidotes. The mixture had a vile scent that made me want to gag.

When I moved towards Viridian with the cup, Jathral grabbed my arm. "What do you think you're doing, bat?"

I lifted my eyebrows, debating on how thick to lay on the sass. "Saving the master of this house. Let go."

His magic darkened around him. "You are walking a fine line."

"You can kill me, if you want, but I have a feeling you need me." I refused to be intimidated by a demon with a god complex.

"You wretched little—" He lifted his hand, and I closed my eyes, ready to take the hit.

It never came.

Jathral let go of my arm. "If you let him die, your life will be taken as punishment." He erupted into flames, disappearing into thin air.

Without his looming presence, I could breathe again. I slumped against the wall and pressed my hands to my chest, taking slow deep breaths to calm my body.

I had thought of Viridian as indestructible, but I didn't know if he'd make it through the night.

Something had nearly killed the powerful demon, and I feared it'd come back, taking more than just the demon's life.

Chapter
10

I didn't leave Viridian's side the entire night. He fell into a deep slumber that made me check on him multiple times to make sure he was still alive. It didn't look like he was breathing in his position, and other than an occasional groan of pain, he looked dead.

A few hours before morning, his body broke out in a sweat, a fever racking his system. Good. The fever would hopefully burn out whatever caused him to be in that kind of state—since the injuries alone wouldn't have done that. Without magic of my own or someone who would admit what happened, I had no way of knowing if Viridian would be okay.

The master of the house was uptight and prickly, but he kept Ethlow running smoothly. He kept us safe. Ethlow would crumble without his guidance, even if his attitude was a constant irritation.

"Long night?"

I bolted out of my seat, facing the grim reaper. Anger flooded my system, but there was also a touch of something else. "Where have you been?"

"Here and there." No one liked to answer questions at the estate, and it was grating my nerves.

I walked away from Astoria and Viridian, needing a moment from whatever was going on. Viridian would be fine while I stepped into my private chambers. I ignored the lump on my bed and looked at the rainbow hornworms. They were all collected around the fruit I had left for them, eating away. In the grand scheme of things, their lives didn't matter, but that didn't stop me from loving them.

They were easy and uncomplicated, unlike the mess I had found myself in. I didn't fully understand what that mess was. It was like I was standing in a pit of darkness with death and danger swirling around me, and I couldn't see the source.

"You did a good job saving Viridian," Astoria said. It was as if her footsteps were ghosts haunting me. I couldn't hear them, but I felt their presence.

I wasn't interested in her praise. "Are you here to take his soul?"

"Not his."

I spun around and found Astoria hovering over my bed, as if mocking the man in it. "Then who?" It was the foreboding question I was desperate and terrified to know.

Her silence was frustrating. No one could tell me anything, and I was tired of it. I stormed out of my room and back to the infirmary to check on Viridian. His fever raged on, making his body shiver.

"Why are you convinced I'm here to collect a soul?" Astoria asked, popping up directly behind me.

This time it was me who ignored her. I grabbed a cloth and wet it in the sink before dabbing the sweat off his forehead.

"Maybe I'm here for a completely different reason," Astoria said when I didn't respond.

"You're a grim reaper, and the demon king didn't invite you here. What else could you be here for?"

Astoria stepped towards me, leaving barely any space between us. Her heat wrapped around me like a warm summer day, making me want to forget my anger and lean into her.

"Maybe I caught a vampire in my trap by accident. Maybe there was something about her that made me want to stay and talk to her. Maybe, for once, I don't want to move through this world to help bring peace to others. Maybe I want to take a moment for myself and just enjoy a moment with someone who is still breathing." Astoria pressed her hand against my chest. She wouldn't feel a heartbeat, but my chest moved up and down with each breath I took out of habit.

Her warmth countered the ice in my veins, and I wanted to lean in and share it for a moment longer.

Astoria cupped my cheek. "Let's dance." Her breath brushed against my lips, making me ache for something I didn't understand.

"There's no music." I glanced at the unconscious demon.

Astoria slid her arm around my back and pulled me flushed against her. She took my other hand and lifted it up. "Then we'll make our own." She guided my feet in circles as if she had spent her life dancing. A soft hum to a song I had never heard before came from the reaper's throat. Even without words, I could feel the joy in the rhythm of her voice. She swayed, smiling at me like I was sunshine.

Heat bloomed in my chest, and my feet were light. When Astoria stopped spinning, my head continued. Her hand slid up to the back of my neck, and she began to lean in. I closed my eyes in anticipation, but then the reaper's warmth disappeared. When I opened my eyes, she was gone, and my chest sank.

A shuffling sound distracted me from my disappointment. Viridian sat up on the bed, his head hanging as he braced his body against his knees. I rushed over to him and gently pushed his shoulders in an attempt to get him to lay back down.

"You shouldn't be moving," I said.

Viridian shrugged me off him. "I'm fine." He stood. He tried to hide his wince, but he couldn't keep his pain hidden. I had dealt with enough ornery patients to know when they were lying to me.

"You nearly died." I reached for him again, but he grabbed my wrist.

"No. That bastard shouldn't have brought me to you. I told him I would recover on my own." He flashed his sharp teeth as he spoke about Jathral, which I didn't blame him for. The demon was arrogant, to say the least.

"You looked like death was calling to you," I said. I wondered if that was how Astoria knew he needed help. Did she feel his soul calling to her and knew if something didn't change, she would have to collect the demon's essence?

"He went against my orders. I should have—" He cut himself off, as if he realized he was about to say something he shouldn't have.

"Jathral is a king. He doesn't have any obligation to listen to your orders." He was a prick who acted like he was above everyone else, so I wasn't sure why Viridian thought he would be an exception to the rule.

Viridian pushed my hand away and stood, ignoring the signals his body was clearly giving him. He straightened his spine and squared his bare shoulders. I had never seen so much of his skin before, so it was strange looking at the toned body that was hidden by buttons and ruffles. I had never realized that the demon was actually attractive.

"You will not speak a word of what you saw tonight to anyone, especially not Nyri," Viridian said in his unbreakable tone.

Nyri was with the demon king, so if she learned about Viridian's attack, she would likely talk to Zathrian about it. "Do you not want Zathrian to know about what you were doing?"

Shadows flickered in Viridian's eyes. "What I do on my own time is my business. I assure you, Miss Satella, that if you tell anyone about what you saw and what you know, it will come back to haunt you."

I could keep a secret. I was used to keeping patient information private. It wasn't my place to tell others about someone's personal ailments. However, there was more going on than a simple stab wound.

"You owe me answers for saving your life," I said, holding firm against Viridian.

The demon clenched his jaw. If I wasn't under the protection of the demon king, I wasn't sure if I'd be safe against the demon. However, I knew Viridian had taken an oath to protect the residents of Ethlow. He wasn't the type to break oaths.

"I owe you nothing for doing your job," Viridian said.

"Just tell me if there is something I need to prepare for. If there are going to be more injuries like yours, then there are preparations I should make." I hoped playing this angle would get Viridian to tell me something. I was growing desperate for any information.

Viridian's body stilled. He looked me over, as if deciding if I was worthy of learning more. "There is unrest building among powerful beings. The future is unknown, but preparing isn't a bad idea."

"What kind of powerful beings?" I asked.

"Good night, Miss Satella." He moved past me, making it clear he wasn't going to answer my question. He walked out of the room, and I didn't stop him, even though he was *walking*. The demon usually used his magic to move through shadows.

Unease twisted my stomach. I had never seen Viridian use his powers to their full extent, but the air around him usually sizzled with power. His strength nearly equaled the demon king's. If someone was able to bring him close to death, then Ethlow was in danger, and I wasn't allowed to tell anyone.

Chapter

II

The sun on my skin burned away the stress from the night. I held Aukina's famous soup in my hands, but I didn't feel like eating. As a vampire, regular food did nothing to sustain my body, but that didn't stop me from enjoying it. Soup was my favorite. I hated chewing, and its warmth filled my belly with joy.

"You're quiet today," Nyri pointed out. She hadn't touched her food, which was unusual for her. Aukina was halfway through her own meal.

I hummed, but I didn't know how to respond. My mind was far away from our little courtyard, but I couldn't tell them why.

"Did something happen?" Aukina asked.

"That's what I want to know," Reamann said, bursting through the door. The sun made his orange hair shine like fire, and his eyes burned brightly. He wasn't good at hiding his emotions. I liked that about him. There were no games with the demon.

I set the bowl down and turned towards the demon guardsmen. "What has your panties in a wad today?"

"You tell me. Iolas is too weak to train. What did you do?" He stopped in front of me, towering over me with his height.

I had barely been able to think about the fae. It had felt like a week ago after everything else that happened. "He donates his blood. He's supposed to take it easy. That's nothing new."

"He looks unusually pale." Reamann wasn't going to back down. He was like a golden retriever to those he cared about: loyal and unwavering. We hadn't grown closer since he and Aukina had become a thing, but that was fine with me. I was happy he made Aukina happy, but that didn't mean I had to be friends with him.

Aukina jumped to her feet, making her long hair cascade around her body. She wrapped her arm around Reamann, and he visibly relaxed. "Satella would never do anything to intentionally hurt Iolas. You know that."

Reamann pulled his lips tight. "I know." He looked at me, his shoulders deflating. "Sorry. I shouldn't have come in heated like that. Iolas not feeling well was the last straw to a stressful night."

My spine went taut. "Did something happen last night?" I tried not to sound overly eager to hear the answer, but it was difficult to hide my curiosity.

Reamann ran his fingers through his hair. "I was called to help last night, because there was an unusual amount of activity around the estate. Usually, the nights are peaceful with *maybe* one creature venturing close to Ethlow. But last night there were at least seven different creatures spotted near the estate, and Viridian was nowhere to be found. It put the guardsmen on edge."

Aukina looked at Nyri, worry flashing through her features. "Did Zathrian tell you anything about that?"

Nyri shook her head, pursing her lips as she thought about it. "No, but I can ask him."

"Last night was probably a freak coincidence with all those creatures showing up, but just in case, don't go outside anywhere close to night," Reamann said.

The air grew stiff with tension, the four of us not knowing what to say. We wouldn't have left the estate, especially not with Aukina's incident a few months ago, but the warning made us uneasy.

"Oh, Satella, how are you worms doing?" Nyri asked to change the subject. Relief washed over everyone, grateful for the distraction.

"Afternoon Tea wasn't moving much this morning, but I think he's preparing to pupate," I said, a smile coming to my face. I loved my bugs, and I loved it when my friends asked about them. Nyri wasn't a fan of creatures with more than four legs, but she always acted interested for my sake. "Midnight Snack and Breakfast Bagel have been eating a lot, so I think they aren't far behind. You should come see them soon."

"I'd like that," Nyri said. I wasn't sure if it was a lie, but I knew she'd come see them either way. "When are they supposed to turn into moths?"

"Soon," I said. After they pupated, it'd be a few weeks before they emerged from their cocoons, but after living for centuries, a week was a small blip in time. "So you had better swing by before they turn into beautiful moths."

Days passed in strangled peace. It should've been a breath of fresh air after the chaotic night of saving Viridian.

But questions burned my throat.

Who attacked Viridian?

Why was King Jathral at Ethlow?

Why was a grim reaper lurking in the shadows?

Why was Viridian hiding things from the demon king?

I tried to ignore the curiosity, Viridian's warning spinning through my thoughts. But I needed to know the truth. There was one place I knew held answers to the world, and I found myself walking into the library, where I spent many nights when a new topic piqued my interest.

"Hello?" I called out when I didn't see signs of Tareen. She was the librarian in charge of the books at Ethlow. She was the only one who attended to the needs of the library, since it was one of the less pressing responsibilities in the estate. We weren't close, but she always indulged me when I was interested in researching a new topic.

"Just a minute!" Tareen called out from the depths of the book stacks. I didn't move, knowing the witch would come to me once she was finished with whatever she was doing.

A thin book sat on her desk near the entrance, gold lettering calling out from the black cover. I brushed my fingers over the dark leather. Between the feel and scent of the book, it was at least three centuries old, if not older. It hummed as I picked it up. It was heavier than I had expected for its thin spine. The pages were worn, but they were made of thick paper that had kept true as the decades passed by. It wasn't written in common. The bold swoops of the lettering belonged to the elves, but it was one of the languages I hadn't studied yet.

I knew multiple languages in the realm, including a vague understanding of the fae language. Elven was one I hadn't gotten to yet, but it was on my list.

"Coming in hot!" Tareen shouted.

I turned, easily moving in time to prevent the witch from crashing into me. Her black dress fluttered behind her as she banked hard on her broom. Her turn saved her from crashing into the wall, but it didn't save her from tumbling into a stack of books.

The librarian sat up, her curly brown hair covering most of her face. She blinked several times with her doll-like eyes, dazed by the crash.

"Tareen, I told you to stop flying. You're going to hurt yourself again." The witch was a frequent flier in the infirmary. Half of the visits were from her weak lungs. She needed biweekly breathing treatments to stop them from failing. The other half of her visits came from various accidents ranging from crashing on her broom to explosions from potion experiments.

Tareen pushed her mess of hair out of her face. "One day I will figure out the secret to the perfect flight."

"Or you will kill yourself." My chest tensed at my own words. I was used to admonishing the witch for not taking care of herself properly, but I had never thought any of her accidents would result in death. Astoria's presence made my words heavy on my tongue.

Tareen pushed herself off the ground and smoothed out her dress. "You have more important things to worry about than a witch like me. I'm just the nobody librarian."

I wanted to slap her for putting herself down, but I wasn't a violent being. I saved people, not hurt them. "Don't talk about yourself like that. You are important to plenty of people."

Tareen smiled, making her cheeks look even rounder. She was short and squishy, which made her absolutely adorable. "You're too sweet. You're wrong, but sweet."

I didn't have energy to argue with the witch today. "Are you hurt?"

"Just a couple of bruises. Nothing serious." Her focus shifted to the book in my hand. "Are you interested in elven history?"

"Oh, this? No. I thought it looked interesting, but I can't read elven." I offered her the book, and she took it.

"It's an interesting read. It's about the elven perspective on the Great Demon War. Many of them were hired to fight, which destroyed their numbers. They became at risk of extinction, so their elders forbade anyone with elven blood to participate in warfare on behalf of other species. Many retreated into the woods and shunned anyone who wasn't an elf. Many even shunned dark elves. It explains why their people keep to themselves, even to this day. They've started opening up in recent years, but only certain clans venture out of their forests."

"I'll have to read it some day," I said. And I meant it. I loved history, especially when there was so much that happened before I was born. Learning about different cultures and wars was fascinating. I hoped I'd see history in the making with my immortal life, but ever since I had arrived at Ethlow five decades ago, it had felt like history was passing me by.

"I have an entire section on elven history. They are some of the early people in the world who preserved their histories. I can show you." She started to move, eager to show me.

"Actually, I was hoping you had information on grim reapers." I grabbed her arm before she could scurry away. She had a tendency to do that. Her mind often went in multiple directions at the same time, so it was important to keep her focused.

"I have a lot about reapers. I have their origins from several different perspectives. I have theories about them in different cultures. There are fairy tales and personal accounts—some I don't believe. I think people just like to tell stories for attention."

"Do you have anything about their job description and their free will?" Astoria implied that she wasn't at Ethlow to collect souls but to spend time with me. I had a hard time believing that. I wanted it to be true. The idea of someone thinking I was worthy of spending time with made butterflies swarm my stomach.

Even if Astoria did like spending time with me, she didn't know I existed until she arrived at the demon king's estate, which meant she was here for another reason, one I was determined to find out.

Tareen pursed her lips as she thought. "There might be something in the special collection. Those books cannot be removed from the library, though."

"That's fine," I said. "I don't mind reading here."

Tareen looked around the room, making me follow her actions. "I can show you as long as you promise not to tell anyone about the room."

Another secret.

If the truth came with another secret, I could keep my lips sealed.

"Vampire's honor," I said, holding my hand over my heart.

"Aren't vampires known for lying to get what they want?" Tareen asked. Her comment stung, but I understood. There were covens out there that lied and killed to get their way. There was a reason vampires had a bad reputation, even if not all vampires were sadistic.

"How about healer's honor, then?" I wanted to believe I was better than the rest of my kind, but there was a time I was just like them.

Tareen thought for a moment before nodding her head. "I can accept that. Follow me."

She weaved in and out of the bookshelves, taking longer to cross through the library. Eventually, she led me to a corner of the library that was shrouded in darkness. There were no lamps or candles illuminating the shelves covered in dust, and the air was stiff. I wrinkled my nose, fighting against a sneeze. Beyond the dust and darkness, Tareen stopped in front of a black door. She reached between her plush breasts and pulled out a thick, gold key that was shaped like a crow on the end. She used the key to open the door.

It swung open seemingly on its own, and a cool draft flowed towards us, sending a shiver down my spine. A dark, musty hallway stood before us, and strange power filled the air. The power within the darkness didn't belong to the demons that ran this place, but its source came from different shadows.

I looked at Tareen. Her expression hadn't changed, but something stirred within her. This wasn't an area she showed to many people, but she had made an exception for me.

"Ready?" Tareen asked, her voice perky and excited.

Nervousness rolled over my skin, prickling the nearly invisible hair it ran over. Ready or not, I didn't have a choice if I wanted answers.

Chapter
12

A ball of light magic floated over Tareen's head as we moved through the dark tunnel. The walls were made of black stone, which only seemed to blend the shadows with the walls.

"What is this place?" My voice echoed off the walls, and a whisper I couldn't understand responded. It was as if the walls were trying to speak to me.

"I have a collection of books and other... artifacts... that if the wrong person got their hands on it, it could cause problems. King Zathrian allowed me to create a space within the estate to keep those items protected. No one can get in and out of here without my permission. I even have wards in place to stop someone from killing me and taking the key."

Tareen and I were friends. We hadn't gotten close, but whenever there was research I wanted to do, she was the first one I went to. It had created a bond over the decades. The witch had been at Ethlow since before I arrived, but she looked just as young as me. Her blood smelled like human with no other traces of a different race, giving her the immortality that seemed to keep her young.

I had never asked how she did it, assuming she either had a drop of blood from a different race running through her veins that prolonged her life or her magic sustained her immortality. I made it a point to not ask about someone's past, unless they brought it up first. We all came to Ethlow for a reason, and many had dark pasts they didn't want to talk about, myself included.

The hallway opened up to a circular room. In the center, there was a table filled with books and loose papers. The walls were covered with shelves. Half of them held tomes with layers of dust thicker than the ones in the library. The others held a variety of items, ranging from daggers to gold medallions to a chunk of black stone.

With a wave of her hand, little balls of light danced on the ceiling, illuminating the room for eyes that could not see in the dark. It looked as if the stars were shining down on the room, which made it seem more magical than it felt.

"Flames are not allowed in here. Most of the texts are too fragile and rare to risk setting them on fire," Tareen explained. Her wild energy had subdued, and she held my eyes, making it clear this was serious.

"No flames. Easy enough." The heat of a nice fireplace would've been nice to counter the cool dampness that seemed to live in the walls, but my joints could suffer for the sake of finding a kernel of truth.

Tareen moved to one of the bookshelves and grabbed two large tomes bigger than her head. She gritted her teeth as she strained to move the books. She dropped them on the table, and a *thunk* echoed as a cloud of dust filled the air.

"These are two of the oldest texts I have. This one talks about the creation of the underworld and the creatures that come from there. This includes the origins of grim reapers. This other one is about the balance of life and death, and if I remember correctly, there are several references to grim reapers in that one."

The books were too thick to read over one night, but maybe with some skimming, I could find what I was looking for.

"I have some other things to do, but when you are ready to leave, just call. I'll hear you," Tareen said. She left the room, and even without her presence, the twinkling lights hovered above me, giving me a smidge of hope.

After hours of carefully flipping through the old pages, I didn't feel any closer to what I was looking for. Reapers were the carriers of souls from the mortal realm to the underworld—that much I knew already. They were often called deathbringers, because they brought the dead to the afterlife, but over the years, the term had been twisted. Many believed the grim reapers to be evil symbols. Towns blamed reapers for the death of their loved ones, but the truth was reapers didn't kill.

That was something.

But after flipping page after page, I found nothing about freewill or why they were responsible for the safe transport of souls. There were endless pages left that might have held the answers I was looking for, but my head throbbed with the information I had sorted through—most of it minimal or repetitive.

My head pounded, unable to read another page. Tomorrow I'd continue. And the night after if I had to. I refused to let myself stay in the dark about what was happening at the estate. I refused to believe it was a coincidence that Astoria showed up at Ethlow shortly before Viridian was seriously injured. Then what Reamann said about the creatures approaching the estate in excess. It was all interconnected. I was sure of that, but I couldn't figure out how.

I needed a break. My brain was too full to think of logical solutions.

I left the tomes on the table and made my way out of the room. My legs wobbled as I walked. After not moving for hours, my body was stiff.

The hallway back to the library had no lights. It shouldn't have been an issue for my eyes, but the walls, floors, and shadows blended together. The floor felt like it was moving with each step, throwing off my balance. I ran my fingers along the walls to keep myself stable, but power buzzed through my veins, calling out to me. Begging me to stay.

I was a creature of the night and dark, and I belonged in the hallway that encapsulated all that.

The urge to sit for a moment washed over my bones. I needed to get back to my room for the night, but if I stayed for a few minutes, it wouldn't hurt.

With the wall as support, I started to sink down to the ground.

A hand wrapped around my wrist, pulling me forward. I blinked away the shadows and saw Tareen's hair bouncing as she dragged me out of the hallway.

She opened the door. Light flooded my pupils, forcing me to close my eyes. The door slammed shut behind us, and Tareen huffed, dropping my wrist.

"I told you to call for me when you were done." Tareen's voice was harsher than I was used to.

I rubbed my eyes to help them adjust to the lighting. The library slowly came into focus, but my head spun. It was as if I had just been in some sort of fever dream.

"What was that?" I asked. The library was dark, no sun coming from the windows. It was late, but I didn't know how long I had been in that room.

"I told you that I have protections set up. That room is designed to swallow anyone without light. It's to stop thieves from leaving with anything that doesn't belong to them." Tareen pinched the bridge of her nose. "You don't realize how close you came to getting stuck in there. If you want to come back, you have to follow my rules."

I nodded, but my head spun. My body was flooded with the strange magic, making it difficult to think. It pulsed and danced in my veins, making me want to move with it. Or sleep. "I think I need to lie down for a bit."

Tareen sighed. "The effects should wear off in a couple of hours, but your senses will be impaired until then. Just don't do anything... stupid."

She walked me out of the library and sent me on my way. The world was brighter as I walked through the empty hallways. The pictures hanging on the walls smiled down at me. A couple of them waved hello.

This must've been what it was like to be drugged. A part of my mind was aware that this was not normal, but the other part didn't care. That part waved back to the pictures.

Footsteps echoed behind me. I smiled, spinning around to welcome the nocturnal resident, but then my back slammed against the wall, a hand wrapped around my throat. The shock sent my brain on high alert, knowing I was in a precarious situation.

I smiled as teal eyes met my own. "I see you're feeling better, Viridian."

He dug his nails into my skin, causing blood to trickle down my neck. "You're walking a dangerous line, Miss Satella."

I giggled, no care for my safety. "I didn't know you were this kinky, Viridian."

"That's master to you." He squeezed my throat tighter in warning, but it did him no good.

I rubbed my thighs together, the lack of control doing something to my body.

"Master," I said breathlessly. "I think I like the idea of that." I wanted Viridian to take complete control over my body. It had been so long since I had been with someone, but I knew what was beneath the demon's clothes. The ridges of his hard muscles were tantalizing.

My fangs extended as my thoughts spun into webs of what Viridian could do to me.

"Are you drunk?" Viridian snarled, flashing his teeth. It was meant to scare me, but it only made me wonder what it'd feel like to have him sink his teeth into my flesh.

I grabbed the waistband of his pants and tugged him closer. "Vampires can't get drunk. You should know that. But I can easily get drunk off you." I licked my fangs, making sure Viridian saw just how long they were. I wondered what the blood of a demon tasted like. I had never had the pleasure of tasting a being that powerful. Fae were the strongest I had tasted so far, but to bite the neck of the *master* of the house.

"You're drugged then." He didn't respond to my flirting, but if I made him angry enough, maybe he'd give me what I wanted.

I slipped my fingers into his pants, but Viridian grabbed my wrist before more than my first knuckles breached his pants. His strong grip made my wrist groan.

"What were you researching in that witch's cove?" Viridian growled. The vibrations from his throat made my core thrum with desire.

"Why should I tell you?"

He squeezed tighter, cutting off access to air, but that didn't bother me. As a vampire, I didn't need as much oxygen as mere mortals. My lungs moved out of habit more than need.

"You should mind your own business. If you push your way into others' affairs, then you will end up hurt. I'd hate for one of my residents to get hurt." His words said one thing, but his eyes said another. He wanted to kill me. He hated that I knew a secret of his, so he had been watching me to make sure I didn't break the oath he forced upon me.

He released his grip enough to allow me to talk. "You know why the grim reaper is roaming the halls, don't you?" He didn't respond. "I know you won't tell me the truth, but if this estate is in danger, I won't stop until I learn the truth. You'll have to kill me if you want me to stop. Or maybe you could fuck me into submission."

A snarl that made the walls buckle erupted from the demon. I waited for him to punish me for my defiance.

Viridian let go and stepped into the shadows. As his body was swallowed by darkness, he said, "This is not a game for the weak, vampire. Back off before you get hurt."

Chapter 13

I stumbled back, my mind whirling. My body had never felt so light and heavy at the same time. Whatever magic Tareen had laced that hallway with made my body feel alive in a way I hadn't felt since the years after I became a vampire. I was aware of the cotton rubbing against my skin. Clothes had never felt so restrictive.

I pulled off my shirt and tossed it to the side, stumbling past my precious bugs. My brassiere came off next. I kicked off my pants before falling onto the silken sheets of my bed.

The ache in my core wouldn't stop thrumming, thoughts of Viridian's hand around my throat feeding the coals aching to be stroked.

I ran my hand down my neck, admiring how silky smooth my skin felt against the soft pads of my fingers. A fire was left in the wake of my touch, but it wasn't enough. My body needed to be touched. I needed that sweet release to stop the thoughts from consuming me.

I cupped my full breast and squeezed gently. A soft moan escaped my lips as my eyes fluttered shut. I kneaded the sensitive tissue, relishing the way it felt to be touched, imagining what it was like to feel wanted. I imagined Viridian's eyes as I pinched my nipple.

I would've let him do whatever he wanted to me tonight. I had never thought about the demon that way before, but he had never had his fingers wrapped around my throat. Maybe it was the magic drugging my system, or maybe a new desire had been awakened within me.

I slid my hand lower, the rest of my body begging to be touched. I slipped my hand past my panties. My thighs fell open, and my fingers slid into the wetness pooling at my core. As two fingers brushed over my clit, the eyes in my head shifted from teal to emerald green. Astoria's laugh filled my ears. I gasped, surprised by the sudden change.

But I wondered what it'd be like for her soft, pink lips to pepper my neck. I caressed my other breast and moved my two fingers in slow circles around my clit, but it wasn't my fingers I imagined. The fingers belonged to the grim reaper.

Her lips had nearly touched mine. I hadn't thought of them before, but knowing I had come so close to tasting the reaper drove me mad. I needed her lips against my skin and her fingers between my legs.

I shouldn't have wanted her. Her presence at Ethlow only meant one thing, and it wasn't good. She was full of secrets, and the first time I met her, she had caught me in a trap. She was a trickster and a liar. I should have wanted nothing to do with her.

But what I should have wanted and what I did were vastly different.

I dipped my fingers lower, pushing past my entrance. I couldn't control the moan that escaped my lips. I didn't want to control it. I wanted to dive deeper. I wanted to set my body on fire with pleasure.

The ache in my core only intensified. It wouldn't stop until I pushed my body over the edge. Even then, I wasn't sure if I would be satisfied until it was Astoria's fingers caressing every part of me.

Fucking a grim reaper was wrong. She was the opposite of me. She dealt with the dead. I worked with the living. She was my enemy, which made it wrong.

But it also made it feel right. I bit my lip, piercing the skin. I couldn't control my arousal, my body slick with the thoughts of temptation.

I wanted to feel Astoria's lips against mine.

I wanted to feel her fingers stroking my nerves until I exploded.

I wanted to fuck her, until...

"Astoria," I moaned. I couldn't get her out of my head, desperate to feel her against me.

"You called?" Her voice brushed against my ear in a soft whisper.

My body tensed as her warmth brushed over my cool skin. She wasn't there. It was just a hallucination. The alternative made my cheeks burn with embarrassment. She had just caught me touching myself while imagining her.

I started to pull my wrist away, knowing I couldn't continue with the reaper watching.

Astoria grabbed my wrist, keeping my fingers plunged deep within me. Her touch felt too real for this to be my imagination.

Her warmth was like the sun, giving me life. Her scent caressed my nose, intensifying the sensations filling my body.

"Don't stop on my account." Her voice was the definition of temptation, but the thought of touching myself while she watched...

She moved my wrist, guiding my fingers back up to my clit before plunging them back to my entrance. A moan escaped my lips, despite my embarrassment keeping my mouth stiff.

"That's my good little blood-sucker." Her voice purred in my ear. "Keep touching yourself for me."

I wanted to hide my face in shame. I had *never* let someone watch me touch myself before. But the pulse between my thighs was too strong to ignore. I couldn't stop now.

My fingers moved on their own without Astoria's guidance. A surge of pleasure ran through my veins.

Astoria's lips pressed against my throat. Her tongue ran over the skin, sending tingles down my spine. Her touch only surged me forward. I pumped my fingers in and out of me, writhing in pleasure. She sucked and nipped at my skin, not stopping as long as I didn't.

I twisted as pressure built in my core. I used my palm to add pressure to my clit as my fingers dipped in and out of my entrance.

"Come for me," Astoria ordered. She nipped my earlobe before sucking on the skin. The mix of sensations was enough to push me over the edge.

I came on my fingers, barely able to push through my orgasm, but Astoria grabbed my wrist, guiding my hand to do exactly what my body needed. My walls pulsed around my fingers, draining me of every last ounce of energy.

I cracked my eyes half open, unable to lift my lids any higher. A blurred image of emerald green eyes filled my vision, but as fingers stroked my hair, my eyelids were too heavy to keep open. Darkness swirled around me.

A hollow call filled my ears. It sounded as if someone fields away was calling out to me.

Every part of me ached, and a drum pounded against my head.

A gentle touch shook me, encouraging me to open my eyes.

"Satella," a soft and worried voice called out.

Nyri's cobalt eyes found mine. Creases formed her forehead, and her lips were pulled tight. "Satella. Wake up."

I blinked several times, feeling disoriented. I didn't sleep as a vampire. There was no need to. "What time is it?" I asked, unsure of how much time had passed. It was unnerving to know I had been unconscious for an unknown amount of time.

"It's morning," Nyri answered. She sat on the edge of my bed, looking at me as if I was about to break. "Are you okay?"

I pushed my body into a sitting position, unable to answer her question immediately. I couldn't remember what had happened in full—only flashes of the night coming to me.

I mentally retraced my steps from yesterday in hopes of figuring out how I had gotten to my bed. I remembered going to the library.

Then Tareen led me to that strange room. From there, things became blurry. I had been reading, and then...

Viridian had his hand wrapped around my throat. A threat.

Then I was in my room, stripping naked. My cheeks heated at the memory. I had touched myself to the idea of the grim reaper.

I touched my chest, surprised by the soft cloth covering my skin. I didn't remember putting clothes on.

Nyri pressed the back of her hand on my forehead. "You're as cold as ever, but I'll admit I don't know what a vampire having a fever would feel like. Can vampires even get fevers?"

I blinked slowly, the gaps in my memory unsettling. "No, not typically. The viruses and bacteria that plague humans don't stand a chance in our systems."

"Are you okay?" she asked again.

I wanted to tell my friend everything, but that was dangerous. If Viridian's threats were real, I couldn't risk Nyri like that. "I'm okay. It was just a strange night. I guess I've been working myself too hard."

That answer didn't seem to satisfy Nyri. "You've seemed a little off lately." Questions burned in her eyes, but she resisted asking for more details.

Around my friends, I tried to act normal. I didn't want to worry them, but I failed. I knew I couldn't tell Nyri everything, but maybe I could give her a kernel of truth.

"I met someone," I said. I didn't have to tell her that Astoria was a grim reaper.

Nyri's eyes lit up. She loved the idea of love and romance. She had been overly excited when Aukina first started dating Reamann. "You did? Who?" She giggled and tapped her fingers together in excitement.

"You wouldn't know her. She doesn't live at the estate."

Nyri gasped. "Wait! Is this the trap lady? What was her name? Astroid?"

"Astoria," I corrected. A small smile slipped on my lips as I said her name. I had imagined her lips thoroughly touching my skin. I had never had such vivid hallucinations before, but the memories stirred dormant feelings in my core.

"I didn't know you had been seeing her." Nyri tried to hide her expressions, but she was bad at hiding her emotions. Her face always had her thoughts written on it. Her excitement made me nervous, especially when there wasn't anything to be excited about.

"It's not like we've been seeing each other. I don't know if she likes me, and even if she does, nothing can come out of it." I looked down at my hands, knowing they were going to be my only source of pleasure, unless I settled for a man.

Nyri pulled her legs onto the bed and crossed them. "If nothing can happen, then who left that dark bruise on your neck?"

My fingers immediately went to my neck, but I didn't feel anything unusual. I jumped out of bed, pushing through the ache in my bones. I stood in front of the black mirror hanging on the wall. I had the mirror specially made out of a sleek black metal that reflected nearly as well as the silver most mirrors were made out of. Silver refused to cooperate with vampires, but other materials didn't have an issue with our reflection.

My make-up was smeared. The dark coal and vibrant green surrounding my eyes blended together and was smudged under my eyes. I twisted my head, revealing a dark, circular bruise on the side of my neck, right where I had imagined Astoria sucking it.

Only I hadn't imagined her lips on my skin.

I hadn't imagined any of it.

Chapter 14

I cleared my throat, needing to distract myself from the thoughts flooding my brain. Last night was a blur, but the flashes of memories racking my brain left me reeling and confused. Was Astoria actually here for me, or was that just a trick to distract me from something else?

"What are you doing here this early, by the way?" I asked before Nyri started with questions I either didn't want to answer or that I didn't know.

Nyri stood, but her body swayed. "I've been feeling a little nauseous. I was hoping you had something that could help."

"I can whip something up for you." I moved to the infirmary, assuming Nyri would follow on her own. I looked through my various herbs and powders I had collected over the years. "What kind of nausea are we talking about? Are you getting sick? Did you eat something bad?" The body required a delicate balance, and different ailments had to be treated in the right way.

"I'm not sure," she said slowly.

I grabbed dried ginger, knowing it was a staple to fight against nausea, and then I heated the kettle over the fire I had going at all times thanks to demon magic.

"Are you feeling sick any other way? A fever, body aches?" I grabbed the jar of honey that I kept for special occasions. Honey wasn't easy to come by at Ethlow, so I avoided using it when possible. Nyri was a special case. As my friend and the demon king's lover, she deserved special treatment.

"I've been a bit tired for the past few days, but I can't seem to keep food down." Nyri hadn't said anything about this when we met up with Aukina and Reamann, but she likely didn't want to worry them. If I wasn't the healer, she wouldn't have told me either. She was the type to keep her problems to herself until she couldn't handle them any longer.

I wished she would come to me before it was too much, but I understood why she did what she did. It was the same reason I hadn't told any of them about Astoria being a grim reaper. They had their own lives to worry about. They didn't need me to add to their problems.

I finished mixing the drink, hoping the general ingredients were enough to help my friend.

Nyri held a piece of hair between her fingers and gently brushed it against her lips. She did that when there was something on her mind.

"What aren't you telling me?" I asked.

Nyri dropped her hair. "Do you think it's possible for me to be pregnant?"

I nearly dropped the cup. The thought hadn't crossed my mind, but it should've. She was sexually active with Zathrian. Certain races couldn't cross-breed, but that wasn't the case with demons.

They could impregnate most bipeds. They might have been able to breed more animal-like creatures. Chimeras had to originate from somewhere.

"If you're asking if the demon king can get you pregnant, then the answer is yes," I said. The thought of Nyri with a baby was strange. I only ever thought about kids when I visited Elcy. The children taught were sweet—most of the time. I couldn't have kids, my body forever frozen in its current state as a vampire. But I didn't mind. The children of Ethlow reminded me of why I was okay without another life to take care of. It was too much responsibility and too much potential heartbreak.

"What if I'm asking you if you think I am pregnant?" Nyri used her hair for comfort. She was nervous about the answer.

Cuts and scrapes were easy. I could heal most diseases. Broken bones were a cinch. Pregnancy—I had never dealt with that. Plenty of people at Ethlow came to me with pregnancy prevention potions, Nyri included. Those who found themselves at the demon king's estate weren't eager to start a family. If Nyri was pregnant, it'd be the first baby at the estate, as far as I was aware.

"When's the last time you bled?" I asked. I didn't have a sure way of learning if someone was pregnant. We would have to bring a midwife to the estate for all of that.

"It's never been consistent," Nyri said.

I nodded slowly, trying to think of other ways to tell if someone was pregnant, but I couldn't think of any. I'd have to take another trip to the library.

"Fuck. Okay." I pressed the cup into Nyri's hand. "Drink this for now, and I'll figure out how to tell. Does Zathrian know?"

Nyri shook her head. "I didn't want to say anything until I knew for sure."

Another secret to keep. "Have you two ever discussed having kids?"

Nyri sat on the patient's bed and looked at the cup in her hands. "No. Everything is so new with him. I love him, but we've only been together for a handful of months. Kids are the last thing on my mind. I don't even know if I want them. And he's always so busy. Some days I'm lucky to spend more than a few minutes with him. I'm worried that if I am pregnant, I'll have to do it alone." Her eyes glistened as she admitted her worries.

I pulled her into a hug and held her tightly. For a moment, all of my own worries disappeared. My friend needed me, and I would be what she needed. I stroked her hair, and soft sobs started spilling from her mouth. "Whatever happens, Aukina and I will be there for you, but I've seen the way Zathrian looks at you. He is madly in love with you. He would drop everything to be there for you and any kids you may have together. I'd bet on it."

My words only seemed to make her cry harder. I held her until she calmed down, wondering how long she had been holding onto her worries.

Nyri pulled away first. She wiped her eyes in an attempt to compose herself, but she couldn't hide her red eyes.

"Let me do some research, and we will figure out answers," I said.

Nyri smiled, but it didn't meet her eyes. "Thank you. Oh, and please don't tell anyone. I don't want rumors to spread."

"Sure thing." I had become a pro at keeping secrets recently. What was one more secret to keep locked up?

It was already dark by the time I made it back to the library. It had been an unusually busy day for patients. Elcy had brought Thalanil to me after he had failed some sort of jump off a ledge and broke his leg. He cried and then begged me not to tell anyone.

Then Wistari, Aukina's best kitchen helper, accidentally burned her hand and needed a salve to ease the pain. She insisted on going right back to work to help Aukina.

Two guardsmen came with different training related injuries—a sprained ankle and a broken finger.

That was all before lunch.

Tiafel—my least favorite resident because of her haughty attitude and rude comments to my friends—came in during lunch, claiming heat exhaustion. It was a particularly warm day for the autumn weather—not that I was able to tell myself. I had to skip the daily dinner hangout with Nyri and Aukina because the stream of patients was nonstop. It left my mood foul, since I couldn't check on Nyri to make sure she was feeling better.

A papercut.

A pulled groin muscle.

Three fevers.

An allergic reaction.

An infected tooth.

By the time the stream of patients ended, it was well past dinner, and I was ready to collapse. It was as if the estate was cursed with injuries. It made me hesitant to leave, even when the stream of people seemed to stop. I waited until it was dark to leave the infirmary. Most residents settled in for the night after dark, since we weren't allowed to leave the confines of the walls. I hoped that meant the freak accidents were over with.

To be sure, I posted a sign on the carved wooden door that indicated where anyone could find me in case of an emergency. I had to go to the library to find out more about pregnancies.

Tareen sat at the front desk, flipping through a book. It was unusual for the witch to be at the front. Usually she was off doing something deep within the stacks of books.

Tareen looked up and smiled when she saw it was me. "I was wondering when you'd show up again. Ready to continue your research?"

My stomach churned at the thought of entering that hallway again. I had never had my state of mind altered like that since becoming a vampire. I didn't like losing control, but I knew I'd eventually go back to learn more about Astoria's intentions. I wanted to believe she actually liked me, but there was a seed of doubt that only grew. It wouldn't have been the first time I had been taken advantage of.

But that could wait.

Hopefully.

"Actually, there was something else I was interested in looking up." I licked my lips, trying to figure out how to ask about the subject without accidentally giving Nyri's secret away. Do you have any books on pregnancies between different races?"

"Why would you need that?"

I kept my face still, knowing I couldn't afford to give away the truth. I didn't like lying, but I wanted to keep Nyri's secret. A white lie was harmless.

"I'm looking to expand my knowledge on the topic. I've never dealt with a pregnancy before, but it's only a matter of time before someone at Ethlow gets pregnant, especially with the way everyone is fucking like bunnies." It wasn't exactly a lie. For all I knew, Nyri wasn't pregnant and was dehydrated or something else.

"I wouldn't know about that," Tareen said flatly. "Nobody has ever been interested in me that way."

I winced, not expecting her response. "I've been flying solo myself, not that vampires have to worry about pregnancies."

"You could get someone if you wanted to. You're absolutely stunning." Tareen shut her book and pinched her lips as she got lost in a thought. "Someone who looks like me can't pull the attention of anyone."

My heart ached for the witch. She was absolutely adorable. Her round cheeks and big eyes made her look like a doll. Her short stature and round body made her huggable. Not to mention, she was smart and quirky. Any man or woman would be lucky to be with someone like her. However, I had learned from Aukina and Nyri that the world often didn't see bigger bodies that way.

Society made it seem like having a layer of fat over the stomach made someone less worthy, but it was bullshit. It didn't make any of them less loveable.

"I'm sure you can, but you're always hiding in this library. You just need to get out there. Why don't you join us for dinner tomorrow? Nyri, Aukina, and I eat dinner together in the little courtyard outside the mess hall."

"I don't know. I don't usually do well with people." Tareen had a tendency to be blunt, so I understood why some people might not have liked her. I found her honesty refreshing.

"Nyri and Aukina are really nice. Just try it out, and if you hate us, you don't have to come again." I was lucky enough to have friends to keep me entertained, but I didn't know if the witch had any friends at Ethlow. I had never seen her outside the library or with anyone else.

"I'll think about it," Tareen said.

"Great. I hope to see you tomorrow."

Chapter 15

Tareen led me to the section that had a full section of pregnancy books. Thankfully, she didn't linger or ask for more details. I didn't want to be forced to lie more than I already had. After grabbing a few books to skim through, I leaned against the nearest wall, not wanting to leave until I was sure the books had the information I needed.

"I'm surprised you aren't doing more research about me."

The familiar voice made me jump, but I quickly calmed my features. I looked up from my book and saw Astoria leaning against a bookshelf, watching me.

My breath grew shallow as thoughts of the previous night flooded my head. I didn't want her to know how heavily that affected me. It was embarrassing enough as it was.

"What makes you think I was researching you in the first place?"

Astoria's eyes glimmered. She liked the challenge. "You went into that witch's cove where ancient magic stirs. Even I can't break through those barriers. Seeing how I am as ancient as they get, it makes sense that you were researching me. I didn't think you were that obsessed with me."

"Since everyone refuses to tell me what's really going on, I have to figure it out on my own. It has nothing to do with an obsession with you." I tried to push off the wall, determined to walk away, but my clothes were stuck. "What the—"

"It's a glue trap." Astoria inspected her nails, a devious grin making her soft lips infuriating. "I wasn't expecting you to fall for it so easily."

A soft growl escaped my lips, frustration pushing away any lingering embarrassment I had felt. I tried to pull free, but whatever glue she used was too strong for my vampire body. "Get me out of this."

Astoria stalked towards me. She plucked the book out of my hands, her eyes briefly glancing at the title before tossing the book to the side. I cringed, imagining how angry Tareen would have been if she had seen the careless act.

Astoria grabbed my chin with her thumb and pointer finger, redirecting my gaze into her eyes. "Tell you what. I will release you from this trap if you admit to your obsession with me."

"I'm not obsessed with you," I said. I wasn't going to admit something that wasn't true.

"Then what were you looking up before you decided to touch yourself while thinking about me?" The reaper's eyes darkened as she leaned in. Her breath caressed my lips, making me want to taste her.

If I wasn't stuck to the wall, I would have run away from Astoria. That would've been better than facing the questions she posed. "I wanted to know why you are at Ethlow. I needed to know if you are here of your own free will or if you're only here to do your job."

"What you really want to know is if I'm using you as a distraction while I'm forced to be at Ethlow." She spoke as if it was fact, but a question danced in her eyes.

"I know you are not here just to get to know me." I spoke softly in hopes it'd stop my voice from shaking. I wanted it to be true that Astoria spent time with me because she found me interesting, but she was a grim reaper. She was from a different world than me.

"You're right." Those two simple words made my heart ache. "I didn't come to Ethlow because of you. I didn't know of your existence before you happened upon my trap."

"Then why bother with me at all?"

Astoria released my chin and broke eye contact. She grabbed my hands instead, carefully intertwining her soft fingers between mine. "What do you want me to say? That I'm just using you for entertainment while I wait for the soul I came to collect?" She leaned forward, and I closed my eyes, ready for her lips to brush against mine. She twisted her head at the last second, her breath dancing against my ear instead. "Would you tell me to leave you alone if I said yes?"

I knew what my answer should've been. I wasn't interested in being used by anyone. Instead, I said, "No."

Astoria nipped my earlobe, making me hiss. "Good." She lifted my hands above my head and pressed them against the wall. My skin adhered to the wall with whatever the reaper used to set the trap. I tugged my arms, but it was no good. I was at her mercy.

Her fingers traced the side of my face before sliding down my neck. Her hand danced dangerously close to my chest. I tried to arch my back, desperate for more of her touch, but I couldn't move.

"You can ask me anything, you know," Astoria said. Her fingers traced the side of my breast, making them feel heavy with desire, but she didn't linger. Her hand moved lower and lower, feeling my side, then my hip. She stopped when she reached my waist band. She tugged at the string keeping my pants up before sliding the tips of her fingers into them. She lingered above the apex of my thighs, making it difficult to focus.

"Do grim reapers have free will?" I asked, taking a stuttering breath. I wasn't sure I cared about the origins of reapers when Astoria's touch was inches away from my aching core.

"Yes," Astoria answered. She moved her hand deeper into my pants, but she stopped before she reached the point that needed her touch the most. "We have been tasked with the honor of escorting souls to the underworld, but we could stop at any time."

"If it's a choice, then why do you do it?" I asked. I squirmed, desperate to get Astoria's fingers to move.

Astoria drew a figure eight on my skin, but she avoided moving lower. "Because without reapers doing their jobs, this world would fall into chaos. We have to maintain the careful balance of life and death to stop the world from crumbling." She pressed her lips behind my ear and sucked on the sensitive skin.

This was not a conversation we should've been having with her hands in my pants, but I couldn't get myself to care about that. I only cared about the softness of her lips touching me.

"That's a lot of pressure," I whispered. There were so many other questions I should've asked, but I couldn't think of any.

Astoria nipped my skin. The sting from her teeth made my body jolt. It spurred the building desire, and I wanted nothing more than to grab her hand and move it a little lower. But I had no control. I was at the reaper's mercy.

"That's why I like to set traps for little vampires who don't mind their own business."

I opened my mouth to argue, but she darted her fingers down, brushing against my clit. A moan replaced my protest.

"Shhh, we're in a library." Astoria brushed her lips against mine, tracing lazy circles around my sensitive bud.

I licked her lips, begging for entrance in the only way I could. She parted her mouth, giving me exactly what I needed. She brushed the tip of her tongue against mine, and I moaned from how good she tasted. It was better than any blood that had ever passed my lips.

My legs trembled as Astoria picked up her pace. It had been at least a decade since I let another person touch me between my legs. It had been even longer since it was a person I cared about.

The revelation hit me like a brick as the grim reaper pushed two fingers into my entrance. I cared about Astoria—for whatever reason. I wanted this to be more than just a distraction for her. I wanted to mean something to her. I wanted to be special.

Because despite her traps and vague answers frustrating me, I felt alive when I was with her. Alive in a way I didn't think possible since my heart stopped beating.

"Astoria," I whispered against her mouth. She hummed in response, her fingers moving deeper. "I don't care why you came to Ethlow." It took everything I had to focus. "But I don't want to just be a distraction. I want to be yours."

Instead of answering, Astoria kissed me deeper, stopping me from saying anything else. She pumped her fingers faster, using her palm to brush against my clit. I wanted to fight against the surging pleasure. I didn't want to give in to her touch until I knew how she actually felt about me, but I couldn't stop the tightening in my body.

Astoria nipped my lip, and then my body betrayed me. I came undone around her fingers. She didn't stop until she pulled every ounce of pleasure from my body. If it wasn't for the glue forcing me to stay in place, I would've collapsed to the ground from exhaustion. I couldn't remember the last time someone had made me feel like that.

I was sure it had happened. When I first became a vampire, I fell into a coven. I spent countless nights with them drunk on blood and sex. But with Astoria, I was completely sober.

Astoria snapped her fingers, and the glue stuck to my body disappeared. I started to slump, but the reaper wrapped her arms around my waist and held me close to her. "You are stunning," she whispered, pressing her forehead against mine. "I can't wait to taste every part of you."

I bit my lip. It wasn't the confession I had hoped for, but it was a promise to see each other again. For now, that was enough.

She kissed me slowly, taking her time. When she pulled away, it was much too soon. "I have to go, but I will be back."

The grim reaper disappeared, leaving me to do my research in peace, but I knew I'd struggle to focus with thoughts of her plaguing my mind.

Chapter 16

I picked out three books on pregnancy based on the section Tareen showed me. Thankfully, they were part of the main collection, so I didn't have to go back to that protected room. I was also allowed to bring them back to the infirmary, where I could read in private.

Before I made it to the door, footsteps clicked towards me. I paused, half-expecting to see another patient desperate for my help. Instead, I saw dark teal hair with matching eyes walking with purpose.

Please don't come to me. Please.

I didn't remember my full interaction with the demon, but I remembered enough to never want to see him again. I twisted the books in my arms to hide their titles and walked with my head down. I wanted to bring as little attention to myself as possible. The sounds of the demon's footsteps quickly approached, making my chest tighten.

The click of his heels unnerved me. Viridian didn't have to walk anywhere. I didn't know much about his powers, except for that he used the shadows to move and eviscerate things in his way. If he walked anywhere, it was a deliberate choice.

Please keep walking.

The footsteps stopped, but I kept going, passing by him.

"Miss Satella." The two words stopped me in my tracks.

I didn't turn around, unable to face the demon after what I had done.

"I see you are feeling more like yourself."

"I am," I said, keeping my eyes forward. He was the last being I wanted to see the content in my hands. He hadn't bothered to hide his distaste for the demon king's choice of lovers. If he thought Nyri was pregnant... I didn't know what he'd do.

"Good, because you are needed in the demon king's chambers."

I shouldn't have been surprised. Today had been non-stop. Why would it slow down just because it was night? But I hadn't been called to Zathrian's room before. "What is this pertaining to?" I should've turned to face the demon, since he was calling on me for help, but then he'd see the blush in my cheeks from embarrassment.

"You will find out when you arrive."

I rolled my shoulders, attempting to reign in my anger. It didn't work. I spun on my heels, squeezing the books to my chest. "You can't demand I go somewhere and then refuse to tell me why. I need to know what kind of supplies I should bring. So either tell me why you need my services or get fucked."

Viridian kept calm despite my aggressive response. His eyes flickered, but not with the darkness that was usually there. Instead, sorrow graced his features. It was subtle, and anyone who didn't know the demon could've mistaken his gaze for his usual serious glare. But I had spent half a century taunting the master of the house, and I had never seen that look in his eyes.

"Who is it?" My voice trembled. If something happened to Zathrian... I could only imagine the devastation Nyri would feel.

"It's Miss Nyri. She collapsed."

The edges of my vision went dark, and my knees wobbled. I nearly dropped the books, but I clung to them, determined to keep all the secrets others entrusted to me. "She was fine this morning."

"She collapsed unexpectedly. Let's not waste time on the specifics." Viridian was right. We couldn't waste time on details.

"Let me grab my stuff." I rushed back to my room and shoved the books in a drawer where someone couldn't happen upon them by accident. I shoved every possible thing I could think of into a bag.

Viridian waited for me at the entrance of the infirmary. I was ready to run to Nyri, but the demon held out a gloved hand. "I can get you there faster."

I didn't think as I grabbed his hand. One moment, we were standing in the infirmary. The next, the world was shrouded in darkness. Shadows filled my vision, too dark for my vampiric vision to pierce. Viridian's hand was the only thing that tethered me to the world.

For a moment, I thought about letting go. The darkness called out to me, and the darkness within my heart answered. I belonged to the night, so it'd be easy to disappear into it. I wouldn't have to worry about secrets or responsibilities.

But then thoughts of Nyri fought off the darkness. She was a light in my life, one that kept me going. Aukina was right next to her. And then there was... Astoria. I wanted to see the reaper again, secrets and all. I didn't understand what it was that drew me to the deathbringer. There was life to her that was missing in my own, and even if nothing came out of it, I needed to learn more about her.

Light pierced my eyes as quickly as the shadows had surrounded us. My stomach twisted and the weight of the world filled my body. Viridian held onto my hand, as if he knew the journey would disorient me.

"Breathe," he ordered.

I opened my mouth and gasped for air. I hadn't realized I had stopped breathing, since I didn't need much oxygen to survive. However, as the cool air filled my lungs, it steadied my body.

Nyri lay on the demon king's bed, her eyes shut. A sheen covered her face, and her breath was labored. Zathrian was on his knees next to the bed. He grasped Nyri's hand with both of his, and his head was bowed, as if in prayer.

I swallowed, trying to push back the dryness that had taken over my throat. When I worked on others, I learned to set my emotions to the side. I couldn't afford to panic or get upset for the sake of the life I was treating. It was different seeing Nyri on that bed, looking deathly pale. I needed a moment to gather myself.

Only a moment, though, because she needed me to be Satella, the healer. Not Satella, the friend.

I shoved my personal feelings into a small box and locked it up. "What happened?" I asked, my voice slipping into my work tone. Calm and collected.

"She won't wake up," Zathrian said. He refused to look away from her, his sorrow threatening to break the barrier I had forced upon my own heart.

"What happened?" I repeated. Dealing with loved ones of the sick was the worst. They struggled to give the details I needed to do my work.

"I came back, and she was unconscious on the floor. I couldn't wake her, and she's burning up." Zathrian's eyes were glassy, but at least he gave me a proper response.

"I need you to move, so I can give her a proper check up," I said. When he didn't respond, I turned to Viridian. "Make him move, so I can do my job."

He lifted a single eyebrow. "What makes you think I can control the king of Kinzlea?"

I gave him the same stare. I lowered my voice, not wanting Zathrian to hear what I was about to say. "If she dies, it will ruin him. I don't care if you don't approve of their union. You will help me do whatever it takes to save her."

He bristled. He wasn't someone who liked taking orders. Even Zathrian didn't give the master of the house orders, but I wasn't going to back down. Not with Nyri's life on the line.

Instead of responding, Viridian grabbed Zathrian's arm. "Sire, give the healer room to work." He had to pry Zathrian away from the bed, but he did it without an argument.

I took the king's place and began my check-up. Nyri's pulse was even, but it was slower than it should've been. Her body temperature was scary high for her fragile human frame.

"Get ice," I ordered to no one in particular. When neither of the powerful demons responded, I dug deep into my vein of authority. "Now."

Viridian disappeared into the shadows, but Zathrian didn't move. He watched me carefully, but I tried to ignore him. I couldn't think about what he would lose if I couldn't figure out what was wrong with Nyri. I couldn't think about what *I* would lose if I couldn't figure it out.

I pulled up her eyelids. Her pupils reacted to the light. A good sign.

Viridian was back in an instant with ice. I grabbed it from him and put it on her forehead. Her body temperature had to come down before it caused any serious injuries. I had seen fevers destroy the brain function of a patient, often killing them.

No. I couldn't think about that.

"We have to cool her down. Her body might have shut down to protect her organs from the heat," I explained.

"Does this help?" Zathrian asked.

A cool breeze ruffled my hair. The room temperature dropped with Zathrian's magic. Between the chilling air and the ice, Nyri's fever lowered. She was still warm, but it was better.

What the fuck was going on with her?

I had never heard of a pregnancy doing this to someone. Maybe her nausea was something else entirely, and I hadn't bothered to look into it, assuming pregnancy was the cause.

I pressed my fingers against my temples, trying to push away the panic.

If I had taken more time to check my friend out, would she have collapsed?

If it had been anyone else in that room, I would've done a proper checkup instead of assuming it was what she self-diagnosed.

"Is she going to wake up?" Zathrian asked.

I ignored him. I had to think. What could cause nausea and tiredness for days? If it was a virus, I could give her potions to ease the symptoms and get her through the worst of it.

But there was only one way to know for sure.

I picked up Nyri's wrist and pulled it towards my mouth.

"What are you doing?" Zathrian demanded, fear and anger mixing together.

Normally, I wouldn't have wasted time answering his question, especially with that tone, but he was the demon king, and Nyri cared about him.

"If I taste her blood, I'll get a better idea of what is going on with her," I said. I avoided tasting patients whenever possible, but in extreme cases, it allowed me to identify the source faster.

Viridian put a hand on Zathrian's shoulder. "Sire, maybe it's best to step away for this."

"I'm not going anywhere." He shrugged Viridian's hand off his shoulder, taking a step forward.

I pulled Nyri's wrist back to me, my fangs extending. I hesitated to bite, remembering what had happened with Iolas. Taking a little too much blood from a healthy being was different than from a sick person. If I lost control with Nyri, it'd kill her. I hadn't allowed myself to have blood since the incident with Iolas, afraid of becoming the monster I once was.

I didn't have a choice.

I pierced Nyri's skin, and her blood filled my mouth.

I spat it out immediately, my tongue going numb. Her blood dribbled down my chin. I looked at Viridian and Zathrian, unable to hold back my panic a moment longer. "There's poison in her blood."

Chapter 17

No one knew how the poison got into Nyri's system. No one else at the estate was sick, and Aukina checked the food in the kitchen, confirming it wasn't some sort of contamination. No one at the green house had seen anything suspicious, either. In the search for an answer, the estate roared with rumors about the demon king's lover. Theories about betrayal and espionage flooded the mouths of everyone.

I shut them out, not interested in theories that did nothing to help my friend. I tried every antidote I could think of, but when morning came, Nyri was still unconscious, and I was no closer to an answer.

Zathrian entered his room, his eyes shrouded in darkness. He hadn't wanted to leave Nyri's side, but he was determined to find the one who poisoned his lover. When our eyes met, he shook his head. He was as unsuccessful as me.

"Can't you heal her?" I asked, slumping to the floor next to the bed. I didn't want to disturb her.

Zathrian shrugged off his coat, dropping his kingly manner in the process. "I can only heal myself. My powers do not extend to others." Anger and sorrow radiated off him, crashing through the room in unbreakable currents.

"Do you know of anyone with healing magic at the estate?" Many beings had the ability to heal themselves, especially the immortal ones, but the ability to heal others was rare.

"Not that I know of, but Viridian is asking the residents. Hopefully someone has a hidden talent." Zathrian sat on the bed, making it dip. He brushed his fingers over Nyri's face. There was such love and pain in those eyes that it made my heart ache.

I had known plenty of demons who took advantage of the weak. Before coming to Ethlow, I had assumed the king of Kinzlea was the same. Even after arriving, Zathrian had been a mysterious figure, looming in the shadows. It was only after Nyri had arrived that he emerged from solitude, acting nothing like I had imagined him to be.

The demon king was kind and caring, and he loved Nyri more than I had ever been loved. I craved that kind of love, but it was hard to feel jealous when my friend lay unconscious in front of us.

"It's my fault she's in this condition," Zathrian said, so quietly I wasn't sure I heard him correctly. The demon would never do anything to hurt the one he loved. "I knew pursuing her was dangerous. I have many enemies, most of them willing to do whatever it takes to destroy me. Loving someone is a weakness, one my enemies will use against me to see my kingdom crumble."

When Nyri had first gotten herself mixed up with Zathrian, I had been worried because of the rumors around Zathrian's last partner unexpectedly dying. After meeting him and seeing how much he cared for Nyri, he changed my mind. It would've been easy to blame him for my friend's current state, but that would have been unfair to both of them.

"Nyri loves you," I said. "She knew the risks of being with you, but she thought you were worth it."

Zathrian looked up at me, his eyes glistening. "If she dies, I'll never forgive myself. I don't care if she thought I was worth the risk. She doesn't deserve to be targeted because of me." Pain I was too familiar with filled his features.

I had been down that dark road, responsible for the death of someone I cared about. It wasn't an easy road to come back from. I didn't want the demon king to face the same suffering.

I stood, knowing sitting by Nyri's side would do nothing to help her.

"I swear to you, I will save her. I don't care what it takes. I won't stop until her eyes open again." My chest heaved up and down, terrified the promise I had made was too difficult.

"It can't be a coincidence that a grim reaper has been roaming the halls of Ethlow right before Nyri was poisoned," Zathrian whispered.

The blood drained from my body. If Astoria was here for Nyri... No. I couldn't let myself go there. "We can't think like that. She is still alive. You have to promise you won't give up on her. Find a healer and bring them here. Bring every healer to Kinzlea if you have to."

"I will do whatever it takes to make sure she wakes up," Zathrian said, but there was no hope in his voice.

The air stirred, a promise between two unlikely friends swirling between us.

I gave the king a single nod. "Call for me if anything changes. I'll be back when I can."

I stood in the mess hall, unable to move my feet. I almost decided to skip out on the dinner meet up, knowing there was work to do, but I didn't want to leave Tareen hanging in case she decided to show up.

A slow breath calmed my nerves enough to cross the room and slip out to the abandoned courtyard. It was a miracle no one else had started taking their meals there since Nyri spruced it up. It was no longer the desolate space it had once been.

Aukina was already waiting for me. She had her arms wrapped around her torso as she sniffled. Reamann wasn't anywhere to be found, which was surprising.

"Hey," I said.

Aukina looked up, her brown eyes shimmering in the reflection of the sun. "Tell me it's not true. Tell me she's just fine, because you already figured out the antidote."

I couldn't tell her a lie. When I didn't say anything, a small sob escaped the mermaid's throat. I rushed over to her and wrapped my arms around her. She clung to me, sobbing into my shirt. I felt my own emotions bubbling up, but I pushed them down, down, down. Everyone else was falling apart, but I had to keep my wits about me. I had to figure out what kind of poison was making Nyri fight for her life. I had to do whatever it took to make sure she woke up.

I had to be a pillar in the unknown darkness swirling around us.

"Should I go?"

I broke the hug with Aukina, and she quickly wiped her tears, trying to get a hold of herself.

The librarian stood by the door, pulling at her fingers. She shifted back and forth on her feet, clearly uncomfortable.

"No, stay," I quickly said.

Tareen looked around. "It's okay if you guys don't want me here. I know your friend is sick."

"Stay," I repeated. "Eat with us."

Aukina sniffled, but she had mostly composed herself. "It'll be nice to have the company. Please don't go."

Tareen sucked in her lips. She looked ready to flee, so I grabbed her hand. I couldn't let her go, not until I asked her questions I needed to.

Aukina passed Tareen some of her meal, and the witch nibbled on the bread silently. I watched the way her cheeks puffed with each bite, mesmerized by the way she ate.

"What?" Tareen asked with wide eyes.

I blinked, realizing I had been staring. "You're cute when you eat."

The witch blanched. "What?"

"You are," Aukina agreed.

"How is the way I eat cute?" Tareen was horrified by the attention on her.

"You look like a chipmunk," I said.

"Thanks?" Tareen lowered her food.

I hadn't meant to make her uncomfortable. "It's cute. It's not a bad thing."

"But now I'm self-conscious about how I eat." Tareen chewed on her lip. "Can we talk about something else?"

It was the perfect opportunity to dive into my questions. "Have you ever made any healing potions or dealt with poisons?"

Tareen straightened at the sudden topic change. "This is about your friend, Nyri, right?" I nodded slowly. "I've made poisons over the years, but not so many antidotes. I might be able to identify the type of poison. Maybe make an antidote, depending. I will need a blood sample."

"I can get you that," I said without hesitation. While Zathrian looked for a healer, Tareen could figure out the poison, and I would...

No, it wasn't time to resort to that. Nyri had time. She was still breathing, which meant we had a chance to help her.

Chapter 18

N yri was stable. That was the only good news. Tareen was working on figuring out the poison used. Zathrian hadn't found a healer yet. I was at a loss for what to do. I had attempted to use every antidote I had in stock, but none of it made a difference. She had been unconscious for two days with no signs of recovery.

I sat next to Nyri's bed, holding her hand. Someone had to be at her side at all times in case her state changed, and it was my turn. I had a pile of books next to me, but I had already scanned them all twice. There was nothing helpful in them.

I didn't know what to do. I hadn't lost a patient since coming to Ethlow, and the thought of losing Nyri was too much. I wasn't sure if I'd survive her death.

It was late when Viridian emerged from the shadows. I didn't look at him or speak, waiting for him to announce why he was there.

"You should go rest, Miss Satella," Viridian said. "I will take over watching Miss Nyri."

I didn't move. Nyri looked at peace in the demon king's bed. "Zathrian was supposed to be the one to take over watching her."

"He is preoccupied."

My breath was shaky. Nyri didn't deserve this. She had only been following her heart, and she ended up in a coma because someone wanted to eliminate her. Ethlow was supposed to be one of the safest places in Kinzlea. It was under the demon king's protection, yet someone had managed to get past the defenses and poisoned her. "Why should I leave you alone with her? You have never liked Nyri. You don't approve of the demon king with a human."

Viridian was as still as a statue, none of his features showing surprise. "What are you implying?"

I turned, careful to keep my voice low. I didn't want to disturb my friend. "As the master of the house, you know the protections placed on the estate. What are the chances of an outsider getting inside and slipping something to Nyri?"

Viridian didn't react. I had expected him to get angry at my implications. "You think someone inside the estate poisoned her."

"What other explanation is there? Unless you're willing to admit you messed up and let someone get to her." Unless Viridian was the one who poisoned her. I wanted to throw the accusation out there, but I knew I had to be careful. If I was right, Viridian could destroy me and any chance Nyri had at waking up again.

"If you're going to accuse me of something, say it. I don't play games." Our gazes were locked in a battle. He knew exactly what I was thinking. The master of the house knew everything.

"Did you poison Nyri?"

"If I wanted to kill the sire's mistress, I wouldn't have poisoned her." Shadows erupted from the demon, his magic leaking from within. "If I wanted to eliminate a human, there wouldn't be a trace left of her."

I stood, putting myself between Nyri and the demon. I knew there was nothing I could do to stop him if it came down to a fight. Vampires were only in the middle when it came to strength and power in the realm. Some demons were below us—like Reamann. I could eviscerate him without trying. Viridian was ages above me. He could destroy me with a simple blink.

"You didn't deny it."

Viridian pulled off his white glove, revealing sharp, black nails beneath. I stretched my fingers, aware of my own claws. "I have sworn fealty to King Zathrian. I would do nothing to harm him or his reign. Miss Nyri is dear to his heart, which means she is my responsibility to protect. When I find out who dared to hurt the sire through his beloved, I will unleash my full powers on them without remorse."

The demon could've been lying, but I knew he wasn't. Viridian had always spoken his mind, and he wasn't the type to hide behind lies. I sank onto the bed and dropped my head into my hands. "This shouldn't have happened."

"No one is as abject as I am. It was my responsibility to protect the estate, and I failed." Shadows flickered off him as he stepped closer.

I knew the demon enough to know everything he said was true. He took his position more seriously than the king did. Even if he didn't care about the residents on a personal level, he had sworn to protect them, and he took his oath seriously. It was easier to blame someone else.

"What do I do?" I asked. I was failing my friend. Just as it was Viridian's job to protect the house, it was my job to heal the injured. I couldn't determine the type of poison; it was something beyond my scope of knowledge, which meant I couldn't create an antidote.

If Tareen couldn't figure out the poison, either, then Nyri would be lost to the underworld, and there was nothing I could do to stop it.

"You do your job," Viridian said. "It's not over yet, so I better not see you give up."

I straightened my spine. The demon was right. There was still time, and I couldn't afford to give up yet. "Same to you. I expect you to find out who did this and make them pay."

"I don't need you to tell me what to do in order to do my job," Viridian said.

My instincts kicked in, making me want to make a crude gesture towards him, but for once, I was grateful for the demon's bluntness.

I planned to spend the rest of the night in the library to continue the search for a miracle, but first, I found myself standing on the roof of the estate. The moon was a sliver, barely illuminating the shadows. My blood was drawn to the darkness, begging me to slip away from the protection of the demon king and let the shadows consume me. I belonged to the night.

I grabbed the edge of the brick wall separating me from the estate and the world down below. For the briefest moment, I had felt free. Astoria had given me a new purpose, one that reminded me of a life outside Ethlow. I had been running from my past for decades, trying to erase the vampire who had given into her lust and desires and lost herself. The one that killed a child without a second thought because the bloodlust had been too strong to allow her to think clearly.

But no amount of hiding could erase that past. I was damned and doomed to live the rest of my life knowing I had taken from innocents.

I was the one who deserved to be lying unconscious with a slim chance of waking up. Not Nyri.

I dug my nails into the stones, not caring as the designs painted by Elcy cracked.

I stood there, staring out at the darkness, waiting. Waiting for the grim reaper to show up, so I could yell at her. If Astoria had told me the truth about why she was at the estate, I could've done something to protect Nyri. Instead, the reaper played her games and set her traps, distracting me from the truth. And I fell for it.

When the sun began to crest the horizon, I pushed myself off the wall, my joints stiff from not moving for hours.

"Stop hiding from me, Astoria." My voice was the only sound as the world crossed from night to day. As the creatures of the night tucked in for their slumber and before the animals awakened from their rest to greet the sun, there was a moment of silence where the heartbeat of the earth could be heard.

I waited, listening for the grim reaper to appear as suddenly as she usually did.

Silence.

"Now that I know the truth, you're not going to show your face?" My answer was like water set over a flame. It started as a simmer, but it was growing into a boil. "Answer me!" I screamed, the pressure too much.

Birds scattered from nearby trees, but there wasn't a word from Astoria. My gut twisted, and I felt like a fool for giving in to the charms of a grim reaper. I should've known better.

As the sun peeked over the distant mountains, I slipped back into the estate, knowing I couldn't wait any longer, not with Nyri's life hanging on by a thread.

Chapter 19

The moment I stepped into the library, I felt the charged energy. Books and papers floated in the air as Tareen sat on a broom, staring at them with a wrinkled brow.

"Good morning," I called out in case the witch hadn't heard me enter.

The magic Tareen was using disappeared. The papers and books crashed to the floor, and her broom dropped. The witch landed on her feet with grace that was unusual for her. There were heavy bags under her eyes. She hadn't slept any more than I had, but her body was punishing her for it.

"I'd say good morning, but I do not believe it is."

The witch's words made my heart stop. I didn't know what she was about to say, but it wasn't something I wanted to hear. "What kind of poison was used?"

Tareen pinched her lips together. Usually, she didn't hesitate to speak her mind. My anxiety spiked.

"I believe the poison is from a hell flower," the witch said.

My breaths were shallow. "I'm not familiar with that." I was familiar with every herb and poison commonly used by healers, but if it had been something familiar, I would've known how to save Nyri already.

"They aren't common." Tareen snatched a paper from the ground. "A hell flower can only thrive in the underworld. There are only a few references to them that I can find, but my magic traced the poison in your friend's veins to the underworld. The symptoms match perfectly."

"What's the antidote?" My voice was barely a whisper, knowing what Tareen was about to say before she opened her mouth.

"There is no antidote. The poison works slowly, attacking the system little by little. Eventually, the body hits a point where it can no longer function, sending the soul straight to the underworld." Tareen stepped forward and reached her hand out, but then she changed her mind. Her hand fell to her side, any sense of hope falling with it. "I'm sorry. I know you care about her."

There was a roaring in my ears. Tareen said something else, but I couldn't hear her. I couldn't move, the news she said repeating over and over again. *There is no antidote. There is no antidote. There is no antidote.*

My hands shook. The witch was wrong. She made a mistake.

I moved, unable to sit still. "I don't believe you." I rushed deeper into the library. There was only one place I wanted to go.

"I'm not wrong," Tareen said. She flew on her broom, unable to keep up with my vampiric speed with her feet alone. "I know you don't want to believe it, but everyone should start preparing for Nyri's death."

I stopped once I stood in front of the black door that led to her secret library. "No. I'm not going to say goodbye." I grabbed the door handle, but it was locked. "Open it."

"There's no point in searching for answers," Tareen said. "Don't waste your time when you can spend what little of it you have left at her side."

I spun on my heels to face the witch. I was tired of everyone telling me what to do. "Stop it. I'm not going to give up. As long as Nyri is still breathing, I refuse to believe she doesn't have a chance. Just because no one knows of an antidote doesn't mean there isn't one. Now, open the door."

Tareen's face tightened. She lowered the broom and dug for the key from between her breasts. "The sooner you accept her death, the sooner you will find peace. Death is a part of life, and she is human. She was meant to find her end sooner or later. It just happened to come sooner."

"There is ancient magic behind that door. We can use it to save her." I didn't understand why she was so willing to give up on Nyri.

Tareen flicked her hand, and the key disappeared. "I can't let you in there in this state. The magic in there is ancient and dangerous. In the wrong hands with the wrong intent, it can do a lot more damage than good. I'm sorry about your friend, but I will not waver on this."

My blood turned icy as I stared at the witch. The hunter instincts I had spent the last several decades trying to suppress surged to the surface. I was hyper aware of the sharpness of my cracked nails and the thrum in the witch's neck. My fangs extended, as if ready for my next meal.

"I'm sorry," Tareen repeated, oblivious to the fact my mind was thinking about every way I could drain her blood. "If I thought anything in that room could help, I would let you in there, but there are dangerous artifacts that could harm many people. I will do whatever you need to help, but I won't let you in there."

Her voice was genuine. She didn't want Nyri to die. She didn't deserve my wrath.

I turned and ran. I ran out of the library, moving through the hallways of the estate, stopping for nothing, even as I bumped into a fellow resident. My fangs refused to retract, aching for the taste of blood. I moved faster, breaking free from the confines of the estate. Wind fluttered against my skin as the sun kissed it.

It wasn't warm. It was the time of fall that was finicky. One day, it felt like summer. The next, it bordered on winter. I wanted the heat to surround me, to drown me until my urges erupted into flames. My feet barely hit the ground before I flew into the next step. I didn't know where I was going other than away. Away from the witch who stopped me from researching. Away from my urges to sink my teeth into her neck or into anyone else I crossed. Away from the suffocation of the estate and the pressures to save my friend.

Caw! Caw!

The sound of the bird made me skid to a stop. The trees blocked my view of the sky, but the first sign of movement drew my attention. A crow circled above me, squawking like a menace.

"Where is she?" I didn't know if it was the same bird Astoria had spoken to, but I didn't care.

The bird landed on a low branch and stared at me with its beady little eyes. It held a silver ring in its mouth with an amber gem set on top.

"Tell Astoria that I need to speak to her. Tell her to stop avoiding me. I realize that I am just her plaything, but she *owes* me." Rage made my vision start to blur. The edges of the world grew dark.

The crow tilted its head. *Caw! Why?*

I swallowed hard. The crow was speaking to me, and I was sure it wasn't my imagination. Astoria had spoken to the crow as if it understood, and it likely did. Crows were smart birds.

"Because…" Why did the grim reaper owe me? She told me I was a simple distraction. She was above the rules of mortals. Just because she touched me, it didn't mean I deserved anything else from her. I stepped forward on unsteady legs. "Because," I repeated, hoping the answer would come to me.

The crow took off, done with me, just like Astoria was.

A flash of silver drew my attention, and my arm shot out instinctively, catching a small, metal item. The crow cawed once as it circled above before taking off into the forest. I uncurled my fingers and stared at the ring sitting on my palm. There was an unusual thrum to the metal, but as I lifted it to inspect it closer, my vision went dark.

I stepped forward, but my body gave out. As I collapsed to the ground, a flash of yellow broke through the swarming darkness, but then it was just me and the shadows.

Chapter 20

When I came to, I was surrounded by warmth. For a moment, I wondered if that was what it felt like to be dead, but it was too comforting. If I was dead, I was sure I'd be deep in the underworld, suffering for my crimes.

I didn't want to move. I wanted to let the darkness fill my veins and take me away. I was tired. Tired of fighting against my natural instincts. Tired of feeling the loss of too many lives. Tired of living.

The scent of basil hit my nose. It was refreshing and pushed away the darkness for a moment. But it didn't stop the shadows from calling to me.

"I can't lose you," Aukina said. The darkness recoiled at the brightness of the mermaid's voice. "I can't lose you and Nyri, so please wake up."

The heaviness in my chest pulled me back down.

"I made you soup. I know how much you love it." Aukina's voice was raw, as if she had been crying.

I cracked my eyes open. Aukina sat on a chair next to my bed, holding a steaming bowl of liquid. The edges of my vision were dark and blurred, but I fought the urge to slip back into unconsciousness. It was as if decades of being alert had drained me so mentally that the idea of letting the world slip by while I slept was enticing.

It wasn't fair to Nyri. She needed me.

The mermaid stared at her hands, not noticing my open eyes.

"I love soup," I croaked.

Aukina's eyes snapped to mine, wide and filled with disbelief. "You're awake."

I pushed myself into a sitting position, immediately making a mallet slam against my skull on repeat. "What happened?" I was in the infirmary with my bugs looking down at me from their frames.

Aukina's hands shook, making the liquid in the bowl slosh back and forth. "You were found unconscious in the forest. Master Viridian said you fainted because you haven't taken enough blood recently. When's the last time you ate?"

Iolas. I licked my lips, a subtle terror from nearly killing him making my throat tighten. I had never felt as out of control as I had the past few weeks. I had canceled all of my usual blood appointments. I didn't eat daily, but I rarely went more than three days without taking blood. A week was pushing it. Iolas had been more than that.

"I've been busy," I said, not wanting to admit the truth to my friend.

Aukina pulled up her sleeve and put her wrist in front of me. "Take what you need."

I didn't like taking blood from friends. It felt like crossing a line. "I'm not—"

"Don't argue with me," Aukina said. "You are pushing yourself to the point of making yourself sick. We already have Nyri to worry about. Please don't make me worry about you, too."

Aukina didn't know that Nyri wasn't going to wake up, but it wasn't the right time to tell her.

"Drink," Aukina ordered.

I took her wrist, my fangs extending as I felt the pulse beneath my fingers. I hesitated as I looked at her tan skin, taking a moment to remember that Aukina was my friend, and no matter how mal-nourished I was, I wasn't about to be the one to harm her.

I bit down on the vein, and her blood filled my mouth. I resisted the gag that threatened my body as hints of the sea drowned out the iron in her blood. Mermaids were my least favorite. There was something about seafood that made my stomach churn.

My body refused to let me pull back, desperate for any blood to give me energy and life—even blood from the sea. The warmth of her slid down my throat, but as the animalistic side of me began to demand more, I pulled back. I swiped my tongue over the punctures on her wrist, letting my saliva help heal the small wound. Vampire's saliva was able to knit together small wounds. It was how we kept our prey alive long enough to feast off them.

I grabbed a roll of bandages out of instinct, but Aukina stopped me. "I don't need you to take care of me. I need you to take care of yourself."

"I'm sorry," I whispered. I felt guilty for worrying Aukina. She had enough on her plate for me to add to it.

Aukina wrapped her own wrist. "Just promise me that you'll take care of yourself."

"I'll do better." It was the best I could promise given everything.

"I'll send Reamann here once he finishes his shift." Aukina stood up and smoothed down her skirt. "You need the extra nutrients, so you can heal Nyri."

My chest tightened, but I couldn't bring myself to tell her the truth. Not when there was one last thing I had to try. I couldn't destroy her heart yet. "Reamann doesn't like me."

Aukina waved her hand. "Nonsense. He enjoys your banter. It keeps him on his toes." I raised my eyebrows in doubt. "He cares about you," she insisted, and I didn't fight it.

Aukina left, leaving me to my own thoughts, but before they could spiral, a noise from my room made my body freeze. Someone was there.

I didn't move, waiting for another noise to prove someone was invading my personal space. Anyone could've gotten in there. A soft click was the only indication that I hadn't imagined the previous noise.

I stood, digging into my instincts to move silently, a predator on the prowl. I didn't like others in my room, especially without permission. The door creaked, breaking the illusion of stealth I had. Pink and purple hair filled my vision. I stopped in the threshold, sorting through the emotions twisting and tugging at my heart.

Astoria stood in front of the glass cages sitting in front of the window. A rainbow hornworm sat on her palm unmoving as she inspected it. She was aware of my presence, but she didn't acknowledge me, as if she was waiting for me to make the first move. My eyes scanned the band of bare skin on her torso, separating her black shirt and matching skirt. The shape of her body was incredible, and for a moment, my mind flickered elsewhere, distraction taking over.

I pushed through those thoughts. Astoria's betrayal was fresh in my heart as Nyri lay unconscious in the estate, struggling to keep breathing.

"You're here for Nyri," I said, my voice low and lethal.

Astoria turned, holding the hornworm up to the light coming through the window. The thick curtains were pulled back, letting the glow of the sunset fill the room. I didn't know if I had been unconscious for a day or longer.

"Life and death walk a delicate line in this world," Astoria said, not bothering to acknowledge my statement. I resisted the urge to interrupt her and demand answers, hoping she'd get there on her own. "I thought you understood that with your penchant for dead bugs."

"I think there is a beauty in the dead. Honoring the dead is honoring life once lived. But death itself fucking sucks. I want my bugs to live their full lives before they succumb to death. I want them to sprout their wings and feel the freedom of flight. I want Nyri to relish the feeling of being loved. I don't want—" My throat tightened, cutting off my words. I tried to tell myself it wasn't too late for the young human, but it was getting harder and harder to believe my own lies.

I took a slow breath. "Why didn't you tell me you were here for Nyri? If I had known, I could've saved her from getting poisoned."

Astoria set the hornworm back into its tank, taking her time to lock it. "I didn't know."

"Do you expect me to believe you didn't know why you were here? With all the games you play, how could I possibly believe you?"

The grim reaper turned slowly, her eyes glowing with power. "Grim reapers cannot predict the future. I did not know your friend was going to get poisoned, and I do not know if she'll live or die. I can feel her soul slipping from her body, calling out to me, but I do not know what the future holds."

"You still could've told me who you were here for. Maybe I could've—" I didn't know what I could've done to stop Nyri from falling victim to a poison with no antidote.

"When I first met you, I was not here to claim a soul. I came to Ethlow because I was tracking another grim reaper who wasn't doing his job." There was an iciness to her face. The woman I faced was not the one whose warm touch had caressed my heart. It was the mask that separated her from the pain of the lives she collected.

She took a step towards me, closing some of the distance between us. Part of me wanted to remove the rest of the space between us and let her warmth fight away the darkness in my heart. The other part wanted to curse her name and tell her to never touch me again.

"And now?" I whispered.

Astoria wasn't breathing. I didn't know if grim reapers needed to breathe or eat or any regular functions of the beings who walked the earth. I knew too little about reapers, and I knew too little about Astoria.

"And now, I wait. If your friend dies, I will be here to take her soul away and help her find peace." Her fingers twitched. The only sign of distress. Or a simple tick that meant nothing.

"Don't take her. Spare her and take my soul. I don't deserve to live, but she does. I will pay the price. My soul for her life." When she didn't respond immediately, I stepped forward. This was my only remaining hope to spare Nyri, since there was no antidote. "Please."

"That's not how it works, my little vampire." Astoria took the last few steps to close the aching distance. "Grim reapers cannot bargain for lives. We do not get to choose who lives or dies. We are the carriers of souls. And even if I could exchange your lives, I wouldn't."

"Why?" I whispered. I was failing my friend, and my chest started to collapse into itself. "I don't deserve to live when I have stolen so many lives."

Astoria reached up, sweeping the tear off my cheek. "Because the world needs you. Because even though the guilt you feel over your mistakes lingers in your soul, it has made you into a better person. You use your talents to save people. The world is a better place because you are in it. Your friends are better because you are in it. If I took your soul, a darkness would fall over this place, and there would be no one to heal it."

"Why do you care?" My voice twisted into a vicious snarl. Too many lies and secrets made it difficult to believe anything the reaper said.

"Because I care about you!" Astoria lost her cool facade. Yellow flames twisted between the green in her eyes. Every emotion she kept hidden burst forward. Fear and anger. Love and hate.

I was stunned into silence. "You told me I was just a plaything, a distraction."

"I asked you how you'd feel if I said that's all you were," Astoria whispered. "Because I was afraid to admit the truth. I am a grim reaper. I belong among the dead, not the living. I shouldn't crave the icy touch of a vampire and her soft lips." She brushed her thumb over my bottom lip, her eyes tracing the curve of them with desire filling her pupils. "I have no right to ask anything of someone I can't promise myself to, because I won't always be around. I can't neglect the souls that need me for the sinful gaze of a vampire. But I want you. I want to throw it all away for a single night with you. For a night of dancing and music. For a chance to pretend my life is something more and to pretend like someone like you could love me, instead of seeing me as a bad omen. Instead of seeing me as a deathbringer."

My heart twisted. Everything she said could've been a lie, but there was a rawness to her voice that made me believe everything she said. "You are not a deathbringer." I dared to reach forward and stroke her head, letting my fingers intertwine with her silky hair. "You are so much more."

Astoria's lip trembled, and for the first time since I had met her, she looked utterly mortal. "I can't save your friend."

"I know," I whispered, the heaviness in my chest weighing down my heart. But as I inched closer until her breasts pushed up against my own, the pain in my chest lightened.

"I may never be enough for you."

I had never heard that much uncertainty from the reaper. She acted as if everything she did and said was perfect, but this was a window into the insecurity that laid beneath her unwieldy confidence.

"Shut up, and kiss me," I ordered.

Astoria's lips tugged up. "I'm surprised you're giving me orders."

Her teasing made my moment of assertiveness fly out the window. "I—"

Astoria tangled her hands in my hair and pulled my lips to her. The strength in her hands made me melt. I wanted to let go and give her every part of me. I wanted to feel her in and all around me, consuming me until I forgot who I was and any worry I ever had.

But it wasn't just a distraction.

For reasons I couldn't fully understand, I wanted the grim reaper. Even knowing she could never be mine wholly, I wanted her in whatever way she was willing to give.

Chapter
21

Heat swarmed me, making me dizzy. Astoria's tongue swiped over my lips, and I opened for her. The first taste of her tongue was better than any honey I ever had. My cravings and desires surged forward, needing to taste more of her. Needing to feel her.

My fingers moved from her hair to the curve of her figure. Her supple body was smooth and soft, making me want to feel more and more. Her fingers moved down until they hooked at the bottom of my shirt. We parted for a moment as my clothes came off, our bodies finding each other a moment later.

She grabbed my hair and pulled my head back, exposing my neck. She nipped the skin right above where my pulse used to flutter. I closed my eyes, loving the pain. I wanted her to pierce my skin and leave behind marks all over my body. Then I wanted to return the favor.

What would a grim reaper's blood taste like? Did they bleed like mortals, or were they above blood and death?

Astoria cupped my breast, feeling the weight of it in her hand as she squeezed just enough to elicit a moan. She pushed me back until my knees hit the bed. I fell, and she tumbled on top of me, giggling as she pressed her hands next to me.

"I think I like you under me." Her smirk left me breathless. If she had been a man, I would've wanted to drain the smugness from his face. But with her, I was a slave, eager to take whatever she gave me.

Her mouth briefly found mine before she moved down my body, leaving kisses in her wake. She kissed and sucked on each breath before moving lower and lower. Her tongue brushed against my hip bones, making me shudder from the surge of pleasure she left behind.

Beneath the reaper, I was completely exposed. I had no control, but with Astoria, it was easy to let go. I was tired of trying to fix everything. I wanted to let someone else take control.

Astoria gripped my thighs and pushed my legs apart. A cool breeze slithered between my legs, but it didn't last long. The grim reaper dove head first into the apex of my thighs. Her tongue warmed my pussy as she tasted every part of me. My body shook as she flicked her tongue over my clit. I bit my lip, fighting against the moans that rumbled in my chest.

Astoria lifted her head long enough to say, "Don't hide those pretty noises from me. I want to hear every sound you make." She stroked her fingers where her tongue had been a moment before.

I bit my lip harder as she circled my swollen bundle of nerves. Embarrassment crawled up my neck as I whimpered from the pleasure. I didn't want to make noise.

Astoria slid her finger lower, tracing the entrance but not pushing in. My body ached for her fingers. I knew how they felt, which only made the cravings worse.

"You know what I want," the reaper teased, watching me squirm beneath her.

My own blood filled my mouth. My need grew stronger. Every part of me craved Astoria. It was just her and me. No one and nothing else mattered. Her finger stopped moving, and another whimper escaped. I was a desperate mess, and her chuckle told me she knew it.

"Please," I whined.

"That's my good little vampire," Astoria purred. Before I could snap at her, she pushed two fingers into my entrance. I didn't hold back my mewls, and she rewarded me for it.

The reaper placed her mouth on my sex and sucked on my clit. Pleasure pulsed through me like never before. Having sex with men was fun, but with a woman, it was enlightening. She knew exactly where to touch me and with how much pressure. She kept her rhythm steady, building the pressure in my core quickly.

Then there was a burst in my core unlike anything I had ever felt before. Astoria lazily moved her tongue until she drained every part of me. My chest heaved up and down as I tried to relax. My head spun, but I wasn't sure if it was from starving myself or from the powerful orgasm.

Despite the deep tiredness in my bones, my body felt lighter than it had in a long time. The reaper had a way of doing that to me.

Astoria climbed up my body and placed a sloppy kiss against my mouth. The mask she usually wore was gone, and her eyes were alight with something new.

I ran my fingers over her curves before sliding them beneath her shirt. The softness of her breast was delicious, and despite the exhaustion looming deep in my core, I needed to return the favor. I wanted to touch her and taste her the same way.

She pulled her shirt off, and I watched the way her breasts bounced free. She straddled me, looking down with her mischievous eyes. I propped myself up on my elbows and took her nipple in my mouth. The noise she made sent heat pooling in my core. I slid my hands down her body until they found her skirt. She was barely covered, but I wanted to see all of her. I tugged at the cloth.

Astoria watched my movements with a predator's gaze. She watched me struggle for a moment before lifting herself off me and pulling down her bottoms. I ran my fingers through her heat, relishing how wet she was for me. I didn't know if grim reapers held the same desires as mortals, but I was ready to find out.

I pushed her gently, guiding her to her back. Astoria clasped her hands behind her head and let her legs fall open. Even though I was the one acting, I knew she was in charge by the way she looked down at me. If she told me to get on my knees, I would. If she told me to never stop kissing her, I would spend the rest of my life savoring her lips.

I kissed down her abdomen until I hovered between her legs. She had such a pretty pussy. I licked my lips, the anticipation only building my excitement. I looked up at her through my fallen curls, waiting for permission.

"Do as you please, my little vampire." Her gaze was intense, watching me with fervor and anticipation.

I licked between her legs, wanting to test the waters before fully diving in. She tasted like a forbidden berry from a far away land. It was unlike anything that had ever crossed my taste buds before.

Astoria tangled her fingers in my hair and pulled me closer. Her patience had run out. She guided my tongue exactly where she needed it most, and I did as directed. I moved my tongue deeper, and her cry of pleasure fueled me to flick my tongue faster. Her body tensed around me, and she pulled my hair tighter. I didn't stop, wanting to give her the same release she had given me.

Her body wound tighter and tighter until the pressure inside her snapped. She convulsed from the pleasure, her thighs tightening around me, but I didn't dare stop until she went limp.

I wiped my mouth before climbing into her arms. She looked at me with a spark in her eyes. A streak of happiness danced in those beautiful emerald eyes before a flicker of something dark replaced it. Before I could ask what thought made those shadows come to life, she kissed me deeply.

"I'm not done with you," she whispered against my mouth.

She waved her hand, and an oblong glass object appeared in her hands. Before I could ask what that was, her mouth found mine, emptying my head instantaneously. Our tongues danced in a gentle rhythm, stoking the coals in my core.

When a coolness pressed between my legs, my body jolted from the sudden sensation. Astoria moved the glass object between my folds before gently pushing it into my entrance. She repeated the motion several times, pushing it in deeper and deeper with each stroke.

The reaper pulled away, her eyes glistening with excitement. "Just relax, my Satella. I'm going to make you feel incredible." She pressed a soft kiss against my mouth and pushed the object fully into me.

I moaned at the pressure, spreading my legs at the sensations. It had been too long since I had felt that full, and I loved every second of it. My hands roamed Astoria's body, feeling her luscious curves in an attempt to feel like I was doing something.

She picked up the pace, moving the glass faster and deeper. The pressure in my body built faster than before, and it wasn't long before I was coming over and over again. Astoria only stopped when the last wave of pressure crashed over me.

My body was exhausted in a different way than it had been over the past few weeks, but I pushed past it, not wanting to seem selfish.

"What about you?" I whispered. There was no one around to hear us, but I couldn't bring myself to speak at full volume. The moment felt like it needed the gentleness of a whisper.

"We'll have time later. For now, rest." She kissed my temple before guiding my head to her chest. I closed my eyes, feeling at peace in her arms.

Chapter
22

I was wide awake as my body was tangled with Astoria's. Her hair covered her face, making it impossible to see if she was awake or not. I didn't know if grim reapers slept, but it was hard to imagine them resting when there were souls to collect. Her bare chest moved up and down in a steady rhythm. Anyone who looked at her would think she was asleep.

I ran my hand down her chest slowly before resting it on her breast.

"Feeling frisky already?" Astoria hummed. She turned over and the sight of her made me smile. In the world of darkness threatening to consume me, she had become a beacon of light.

"I was just curious if you were awake." I stroked gentle circles on her chest, making her nipple pebble from the sensation.

She hummed in disbelief. "If you want me again, you can just say so." She rested her palm against my stomach. Her warmth seeped into me, and I was content. I would've been content to just lie there with her if there weren't other pressing matters.

I needed to check on Nyri before continuing my search for a cure. As long as she was alive, I refused to give up on her, no matter how grim things looked.

Astoria pushed my curls out of my face. "You're thinking about your friend."

It wasn't a question, but I nodded anyway. I should've been at the library doing research. Or going into town to look for a healer. Or anything other than lying in bed. But as I thought about what I should have been doing, my body grew heavy with burdens.

"You can save her," Astoria said.

I blinked twice. I must've heard her wrong. "What?"

"There is a path that leads to her survival."

I didn't breathe, afraid to get my hopes up. "I thought you couldn't see the future. I thought you said you only felt her soul calling to you."

Astoria sat up. "The future isn't set in stone. I can't see what will happen, but I feel different paths. There are some where your friend dies, and there are some where she lives."

I sat up to match her gaze. "How?" My chest buzzed with a new life. If there was any hope of saving Nyri, I'd find it.

"I don't know," Astoria said. "I can't see specifics. Just like how I couldn't see that he was going to poison her, I can't see how you can save her."

My entire body tensed. "He? You know who poisoned Nyri."

Astoria disappeared from the bed, reappearing several feet away. She began pulling her clothes on, as if she was delaying answering me.

"Astoria?"

Shame stained her face. She pinched her lips together and took a visible breath. "The grim reaper I tracked here... I think he did it. I don't know why."

"I thought grim reapers aren't supposed to mess with mortal lives."

"We're not." Astoria's shoulders dropped. "This grim reaper went rogue, so I've been hunting him, trying to stop him, but he keeps slipping through my fingers. He came to Ethlow, and I don't know why, but it seems he is trying to usurp Zathrian's power. First, he went after his second in command. Then his lover."

"How long have you known this?" I couldn't move as I stared at the woman in front of me. She had trapped my heart without me realizing it, but there was so much I didn't know about her.

"Telling you the truth of why I was here would have only put you in danger," Astoria said. Her features hardened. "I wanted to protect you, because if you knew and got hurt because of that knowledge, I would never forgive myself. If he learned that I truly cared for you—" She shook her head. "Promise me you won't look for him."

I studied the mask Astoria had put on. It would have been easy to call her a liar and tell her to leave, but I chose to believe her. I had been warned multiple times not to look for more information. Viridian understood how dangerous this other grim reaper was and swore me to secrecy to protect me from getting more involved. Astoria used her games and tricks to keep me from the truth.

All to protect me.

"I promise." It was easy to promise to stay out of that. "But I will find a way to save Nyri, no matter the cost."

Astoria was in front of me a moment later. She took my hands in hers. "Promise me you'll be careful."

I nodded, even though I wasn't sure I could keep that promise. I pulled her in for a kiss for one last taste before my search for a way to save Nyri continued.

A knock on my door interrupted the kiss. Astoria disappeared, and I rushed to put on my clothes. As I reached for the door handle, I expected Reamann's fiery hair to greet me, but it was Zathrian who stood in front of my door. His face was hard, which made my body go taut.

"Is she—?" I couldn't finish my question. If Nyri had faded while I indulged in the touch of a grim reaper...

Zathrian shook his head. "She's hanging on, but barely. Another healer is inspecting her, but you should come."

I didn't like his tone. It made me want to slip back into my room and pretend everything was okay, but I couldn't run away from this.

I followed Zathrian through the estate, neither of us speaking. It was difficult to make light conversation when a person we loved was fighting for her life, and there was little we could do to help. When we were close to the door that led to Zathrian's room, a strange scent hit my nose.

My feet stopped moving, remembering that scent. Apples and pine. It had been a scent in my life for decades, right up until my life burned around me. Zathrian opened the door, and the scent grew stronger. I didn't want to believe it to be true. Apples and pine weren't uncommon scents. It was merely a coincidence that the smell filled Zathrian's room.

Except I didn't believe in coincidences.

A woman wearing a thin dress that showed off her long and muscular legs stood next to the bed. Her hair was twisted into dark green braids, just as it had been the last day I had seen her. She turned, her nearly black eyes piercing my soul with a single look. Her dark skin looked as if she hadn't changed a day since I'd last seen the nymph.

Axilya smiled, recognition flooding her face. "Satella, my dear. I'm surprised to see you're still alive."

Zathrian looked between us, quickly realizing this wasn't the first time we had met. "How do you two know each other?"

"I was Satella's mentor until she abandoned me," Axilya responded.

My fangs extended, and I ran my tongue over the points, wondering how it would feel to rip the nymph's life away. "We had different ideas about what healing meant." That was an understatement, but I wasn't interested in going into the details of what happened. I turned to the demon king. "She shouldn't be here. She won't do any good for Nyri."

Axilya sat on the bed and brushed Nyri's hair out of her face. I stretched my fingers, ready to destroy my nails if the woman did anything to harm my friend.

Zathrian looked back and forth between us, unsure of how to handle the situation.

"This woman was poisoned by a hell flower," Axilya said. "There is no antidote to such poison, even among the nymphs." Nymphs were known for their connection to nature. Their magic revolved around it. It was why I chose to study under a nymph healer. Axilya knew what plants were best for healing sickness, tending to wounds, soothing pain. She was my greatest teacher of all time.

"We already know that," I said with a tight voice. I didn't need the reminder.

"I'm not surprised. You were always my star student." The nymph stood and faced the demon king. "There is a way to save your mate."

Zathrian's eyes glowed, but no other part of him moved. "How?" he whispered, as if he was afraid to believe the words of the nymph.

Nymphs were liars and schemers. I had learned that the hard way.

Axilya turned to me. "Satella knows how." The corner of her lip twitched up. Triumph filled her face, and I knew exactly how I could save Nyri.

"No." I kept my voice firm as I had the first time the nymph had suggested something like that.

"Surely you remember what we discussed." Axilya sauntered over to me, swaying her hips in that way that made most men succumb to her whims.

"I remember," I said coldly. "But I won't do it." There were lines I had drawn long ago that I refused to cross.

"I don't understand," Zathrian said. "If there's a way to save her, why won't you do it?"

"Because I won't turn someone into a vampire—especially when they don't have a say in the matter." Axilya knew this was my line, but that had never stopped her from pushing me to do it anyway.

"Vampires are immune to poison," the nymph continued. "And they have incredible healing abilities. If Satella turns Nyri into a vampire, the poison will be destroyed by the vampiric virus."

"If it'll save her—" Zathrian began.

"There is no guarantee it will save her." I couldn't let him get his hopes up. "The transformation is not easy, and she's weak. The transformation could kill her faster."

"But if there's a chance, wouldn't you want to save your friend?" Axilya smiled like a feline.

It made me want to strangle her. "I was turned into this against my will, and I spiraled. The urges of a new vampire are uncontrollable. I killed a lot of people from the bloodlust that took over my senses. Innocent people. Powerful people. Children. It didn't matter. I barely had control, and I hated myself for it. I won't put that curse on Nyri, even if it means saving her life. I won't turn her into a soulless monster." I walked away, turning my back on the demon king and my friend.

Chapter 23

Autumn's changing grip had officially taken over the land. The icy wind that yanked the leaves off the red and orange trees was proof of that. I refused to let my body shiver as I stared at the world beyond Ethlow, at the shadows that moved over and through it. The pull of the darkness moved through my veins and wrapped around my heart.

But it wasn't a call to darkness. It was a warning.

The changes around the demon king's estate weren't coincidences. The creatures that emerged through the thin veil between the underworld and the mortal realm didn't wander to Ethlow aimlessly. Grim reapers didn't poison humans without reason, and powerful demons weren't provoked accidentally.

I didn't understand *why* any of this was happening. Only that Nyri had been unfairly caught in the crossfire. She was left without the official protection of the demon king, which left her vulnerable to attacks. Demons were able to mark their chosen mates with a powerful seal that warned others not to go near them. Aukina had a mark like that on her neck from Reamann. Nyri deserved that protection even more.

But a council of powerful demons restricted Zathrian's power, saying he didn't deserve a protected mate because of a mistake he had made long before Nyri was born.

Now, she was suffering because of it. I could possibly save her if I crossed the line I had drawn over a century ago. I couldn't get Zathrian's face out of my head. He had looked so hopeful, and I shattered that.

Nyri could live.

If I broke the one rule I had set for myself.

"I'm surprised to find you out here when it's so cold." Astoria appeared on the wall next to me. Her warmth seeped into my skin, fighting against the autumn chill.

"Vampires were meant to thrive in the cold and the night," I said.

Astoria slid over, a frown painting her face. "Yes, but you don't like the cold."

"That's because I hate being a vampire." I wasn't sure if I had ever said those words out loud before. I never wanted others to know just how much I hated myself, so I smiled and teased, hiding the truth for the lonely nights. With Astoria, it was different. I wanted her to see every part of me, because I wasn't afraid of her judgment.

"Why?" No harshness in her tone. Just curiosity.

"Because I'm a soulless leech who sucks the blood of others for her own survival." And if I decided to save Nyri, she would become the same thing.

Astoria leaned to the side, forcing me to meet her eyes. "You're not soulless. If anyone would know that, it's me."

I blinked twice. "Everything I have ever read describes vampires as hell monsters who escaped from the underworld to wreak havoc on the living. We are considered to be living dead."

Astoria grabbed my chin. "You're not soulless, and you're not a monster."

"I feed off others' life force." I breathed deeply, taking in the grim reaper's scent. She felt like a new beginning, one with happiness and peace. "How can I be anything but a monster?"

"Would you call Nyri a monster? She eats animals. She survives off the life force of creatures."

"That's different." The humans in the town I ravished had tried to burn me after I killed their friends and family. Their screams of pain and horror haunted me on my lonely night walks.

"You're right. You don't kill to eat. You take what you need, and then let them go on their way *alive*." Astoria brushed her thumb over my lip, distracting me and pulling me from the depths of my thoughts.

"I've killed before." It had been a long time since that happened, but I'd never forget their faces.

"And? We all make mistakes. What matters is you learned from it and changed." She brushed her lips against the side of my mouth. It would've been easy to get lost in her touch and use it as a distraction, but I couldn't waste time.

"I can save Nyri if I change her into a vampire." I waited for the excitement to fill her face just as it had with Zathrian.

Instead, she tilted her head. "Are you going to do it?"

"I swore I would never change anyone into a vampire. Even if I change my mind, I can't change someone without her permission. I know too well how that feels, and I couldn't put that burden on her shoulders. If she woke up and gave me permission, I would consider changing my mind, but as is, I won't do it." I squeezed my eyes shut, wondering if the demon king would blame me for the death of his lover. Would he kick me out of Ethlow for it?

Astoria held my hands silently. She waited for me to sort through my thoughts.

When I opened my eyes, I felt calmer, but there was still too much on my shoulders. "If I don't change Nyri, does that mean I'm killing her?"

"No," Astoria said without hesitation. "There is only one person who will be responsible for her death."

I pinched my lips together. She said exactly what I needed to hear, but it didn't help. Even if I wasn't the one who poisoned her, it felt as if her life was in my hands. I didn't know if I could forgive myself if I let her die, and I didn't know if I could live with myself if I turned her into a vampire against her will.

Astoria pressed her lips against my temple. "You'll make the right decision."

"How do you know?"

"Because I can see your soul, little vampire, and I know you'll do what you think is best. That is all anyone could ask of you." She pressed her lips against mine, and for a moment, I let the reaper distract me from the reality of the situation.

I sat by Nyri's bed for the rest of the night, wishing I could hear her thoughts. Zathrian was nowhere to be seen. He spent less and less time next to her. It wasn't that he cared less. He had only grown more desperate to find a way to save her life. Where he went, I didn't know. I didn't ask him or the others what they were doing, because I knew they were doing everything in their power to save her life.

Unlike me.

"Would you pay the price to keep living?" I asked Nyri. I knew she wouldn't answer, but there was a small part of me that hoped otherwise. "Would you become a creature of the night to be with Zathrian forever?"

Her pulse had weakened. I didn't know if she had days or weeks left. Either way, it was too short.

I extended my fangs, thinking about what it would be like to transform her.

"Please," Zathrian whispered, making me jump. He stood in the shadows of the room, watching me with his glowing yellow eyes. His power pulsed in the air, strong and chaotic. He was one of the most powerful demons I had ever come across, but he couldn't do anything to save the woman he loved.

His hopelessness weaved in and out of his magic.

"I will do anything you desire to save her. I will give you power and magic if you turn her to save her." A demon's true strength came from the deals he made. He could give me wealth and power. He could grant powers beyond my imagination or kill for me. But he couldn't save the one he loved, no matter the deal he made.

Zathrian emerged from the shadows with glassy eyes. As he moved across the room, I didn't see a powerful demon king. I saw a broken male who was losing the love of his life. He dropped to his knees in front of me.

Usually, I enjoyed the sight of a male on his knees, but I hated the sight of him like that, knowing it was my friend that made him vulnerable.

I moved to my knees in front of him. I wrapped my arms around his torso, barely able to get my arms around his muscular chest. "I'm sorry," I whispered. Despite knowing I could save Nyri by injecting her with my vampiric venom, I knew I couldn't do it—not without her permission.

A sob broke from the demon king, and I held him tighter, trying to take away as much pain as I could. There was still time to find a way to save Nyri, and I refused to give up. Zathrian held me tightly, sobbing into my neck, and I didn't move until he had calmed down hours later. When was the last time the demon king had let himself be so vulnerable?

I left him in the quiet night to look after Nyri, knowing he would take good care of her while I continued my search. There had to be something I was missing.

As I stepped into the dark hallway of the estate, the shadows moved. I expected the teal eyes a second before they pierced my soul.

"I have never seen him this desperate before. You could've taken everything from him," the master of the house said, making it clear he had been watching us. "I'm surprised you didn't."

I sneered at the demon. "I have no intention of taking advantage of the king, not when he has given me sanctuary for decades." I pushed past the demon, ready to storm off, but he grabbed my arm.

He looked down at me with a gaze that would crumble the weak. "Thank you."

I stopped fighting him, surprised by his words. He hadn't thanked me when I saved his life, but he thanked me for that.

"If you're truly grateful, you'll tell me why you were fighting a grim reaper."

Viridian's grip tightened. If he squeezed any harder, he could snap my arm. "I thought I told you to stay out of it."

"He poisoned Nyri. Is that why you fought him?" I knew I was crossing a line, one that I should've stayed far away from, but I was tired of the secrets.

Viridian tensed, death flashing through his eyes. "I don't know what you're talking about."

"Don't lie to me," I snapped. "You told me to prepare for more injuries. Tell me why."

The ire in his eyes bordered on pure rage. There was a debate going on in his head about whether it was worth breaking his oath to kill me.

"The kingdoms have been at peace for a millennium," Viridian finally said. "But unrest is beginning to stir. There are those who want to destroy that peace, which means King Zathrian and Ethlow could become a target. I am doing whatever it takes to stop that from happening. That is all I will tell you, so consider us even."

Chapter 24

The greenhouse felt empty without Nyri's presence. Even the plants drooped without her magic coaxing life into them. Two gardeners worked to upkeep the plants, but without their leader, their movements were slow. It was as if the entire estate felt Nyri's absence. She was the newest resident, but she had made an unpredictable impact on everyone.

Aukina walked next to me, nibbling on her lunch. We couldn't bring ourselves to go back to the little courtyard. Without Nyri's presence, it felt too heavy. The greenhouse wasn't much better.

"Reamann suggested we take a day off and go to the lake to get our minds off everything," Aukina said. "You could come with us, if you want."

A day in the sun before winter sounded incredible, but I knew I couldn't leave. "I need to stay close to Nyri." She was fading fast. It made me want to tell Aukina to stay, but she had spent nearly every moment of her free time bringing Nyri food she never ate. She had lost some of her rich color, and it worried me. It would be good for the mermaid to get away for a day and enjoy her sea form.

Aukina stopped as we reached the back of the greenhouse. The area was off limits to regular residents, but since Nyri was in charge of the greenhouse, she had taken us back there multiple times. The mermaid hesitated without Nyri's presence.

I pushed the curtain to the side and took in the bleeding heart lilies lining the wall. The flowers behind the curtain were delicate things. They died when a breeze hit them wrong, but Nyri held magic that spoke to plants. Zathrian had gifted her one of the expensive flowers, and over the summer, she had made the flower multiply.

I moved closer, not daring to touch the bleeding heart lilies. The white petals curled in a way that made them look like hearts while red tendrils flowed from the center, mimicking a stream of blood. Most of the flowers were a simple white, but the one in the corner had royal purple petals with streams of gold spewing from it—a rare variant according to Aukina. The mermaid grew up in the sea by the Nescen Islands, where the flowers originated.

"Who will take care of the flowers if Nyri doesn't make it?" Aukina asked.

The bleeding heart lilies were Nyri's pride and joy. It was as if they were her children, and she always talked about how well they were doing.

"Don't talk like that," I said. "Nyri will wake up."

It felt like a lie, but I refused to speak about a future she wasn't in. I had spent days in the library, barely leaving other than to feed and see Astoria, but there was nothing in the books that seemed to help.

"Maybe we should start preparing for the worst." Aukina's voice was raw. It wasn't easy for her to say that. I knew that, but I couldn't stop my rage from boiling in my chest.

I took a slow breath, knowing it wasn't fair to take my anger out on Aukina. She wasn't the one I was mad at. I was mad at the one who poisoned her. I was mad at the world for letting cruelty come to someone so innocent. I was mad at myself for not being willing to cross the line to save her.

The bleeding heart lilies swayed, but there was no breeze inside the glass walls that housed them. The air buzzed, as if they were calling out with a tendril of magic. I glanced at Aukina to see if she felt the same change as me. Her brows were furrowed.

"It's like they are singing to us," Aukina said.

I held still and listened. The noise was soft, and almost sounded like rustling, but as I focused on it, there was a rhythm to it. The sounds rose and fell like a voice weaving a story.

I stepped closer. I had never heard anything like it. "I think the flowers have magic."

Aukina moved closer, but she wrapped her arms around her torso beneath her chest, pushing her breasts together accidentally as she tried to keep her fingers to herself. "The islanders always said the flowers were magical, but I thought they meant it in the way a sunset is magical."

The singing increased, and I didn't have to strain to hear it. I couldn't understand what the flowers were saying, but I felt a surge of energy. The answer to what was happening lay on the tip of my tongue. Then it hit me.

"Didn't Nyri say something about witches thinking the flowers had healing abilities?" I asked.

Aukina's eyes widened. "I think so, but wouldn't Tareen have known about that?"

"As a healer, I have never heard that. It's not common knowledge, but if there's a chance—" No. I couldn't get my hopes up.

Aukina and I shared a glance. A glimmer of hope filled the air as the flowers swayed, calling to us. Would Nyri's beloved flower be the thing that saved her?

"Let's go." I grabbed Aukina's hand and dragged her out of the greenhouse and to the library. I slowed when I heard the mermaid's strained breathing, forgetting for a moment that her mortal body wasn't used to running on land.

We burst into the library, stopping only to look for Tareen in the main area. When she wasn't there, I shouted, "Tareen!" I waited for her to call back, but when she didn't, I continued pulling Aukina through the stacks of books.

I weaved in and out of the shelves, looking for the witch's wild hair. I called her name, waiting for her to respond in that chaotic way she usually did, but only silence responded. As we moved through the bookshelves without Tareen for a guide, it felt as if the ground changed beneath us, making the library stretch and grow in ways that left me confused. I didn't stop, a new fervor burning my bones.

The rows of bookshelves ended abruptly, revealing the thick black door that led to the forbidden area of the library. The door opened, and Tareen slipped out. When she saw us, she let go of the handle, and the door slammed shut. She stared at us with her big brown doll-like eyes.

"Hello." Confusion laced the single word, as if she hadn't expected anyone to be so deep in the library. "How did you get here?"

I let go of Aukina's hand and stepped close to Tareen. "Nevermind that. I need to know everything you know about bleeding heart lilies. Any literature you have on them, we need to go through it now."

"Why do you want to know about some flower so urgently?" Tareen began moving, and I followed her with ease. She slid between the bookshelves, turning left, then left, then left again. We should've ended up back at the black door, but it was nowhere to be seen.

"Because we think we can use the flower's magic to heal Nyri," Aukina answered. She pressed her hand against her chest, her ribs heaving up and down as we kept pace with the witch.

"The bleeding heart lily isn't used as a healing herb," Tareen said. She plucked a book off the shelf.

"That doesn't mean it can't be," I said. I wasn't looking for a known way to heal a hell flower's poison, because there wasn't any.

"If there was a way, I would've heard of it." Tareen paused to pluck a book off the shelf with an invisible hand.

"Not unless the flower is so rare that no one dared to experiment with it," I pointed out. There were plenty of things in the world that people didn't know.

The witch paused, taking in my words. "You're right," she said after a moment. "I will see what I can find out about the flower.

I might be able to make a tonic, but I don't usually make healing potions. My potions tend to have a more... lethal nature."

"I know someone who could help," I said, knowing I didn't like the solution. But I would do whatever it took to help Nyri.

I was familiar with brewing healing potions, but if we were going to use a flower as rare as the bleeding heart lilies, then I wanted an expert by my side. I needed Axilya.

I strummed my fingers against the wood, waiting for the nymph to finish her food. When she was done, she set her fork down gently and looked at Aukina. "You are an incredible cook. It's a shame you are wasting your talents here when you could be earning pockets full of gold with other nobles.

Aukina smiled, the compliment shifting her entire mood. "Thank you, but I'm happy serving the demon king."

"There are other demon rulers that would actually pay for your skills. Don't settle." The nymph flicked her eyes at me in a taunt. She had told me I was settling instead of exploring my abilities countless times. She knew how to get under my skin and how to push me.

"Respectfully, I'm not settling," Aukina said.

"Are you going to help us or not?" I snapped, losing my patience.

"There's a lot of pressure to heal the king of Kinzlea's chosen mate." She took a long sip of her drink. She wanted me to give her a reason to help, but I already knew she would. If not for the glory, then for the love of healing. Despite our different ideas of what lengths a healer should go through to heal a person, Axilya always had the health of her patients in mind. In that sense, she was a better healer than I ever could have been.

"Would you really give up the chance of experimenting with a bleeding heart lily? I'm sure you know as well as I do that those flowers do not normally grow in Kinzlea, let alone the rest of the continent." If Axilya needed me to do the song and dance, I would. If it meant finding a way to save my friend, I would swallow my hatred for the nymph and work with her.

"You could become the first to ever discover the healing nature of the flower," Aukina added. She picked up on Axilya's ego and knew it needed a stroke.

The nymph set her cup down after a long moment of silence. "I will get the credit for the discovery." A selfless healer who selfishly wanted glory.

"Fine," I agreed without hesitation. If I wanted glory, I wouldn't have slipped away from the world, hiding in Ethlow for decades.

"And I want to borrow Satella for a week every year to work as my apprentice." Axilya met my eyes, knowing this ask was one of the hardest things for me to agree to.

For Nyri's sake, I should've agreed. A week was nothing for an immortal vampire, but the thought of the nymph stealing me for whatever nefarious activities was unbearable.

"You may study with me at Ethlow for a week each year, with King Zathrian's approval," I countered. I stared back at her. The nymph knew me well enough to know when I wouldn't budge.

Her eyes flickered with approval. "I supposed that will be acceptable. When do we start?"

Chapter 25

Every order Axilya gave, I followed without hesitation. It was like the old days when I worked as her assistant. We saved countless lives, especially when a dark disease struck the human lives of Kinzlea. We brewed tonics to clear their airways and give their bodies the energy to survive the disease. We mended bones, granted women the gift of fertility, and so much more. I had learned almost everything I knew as a healer during my time with the nymph, and each life we saved made up for a sliver of the damage I had done.

Then she decided we could save more lives if we explored the possibilities of the vampiric virus. I had said no, and she dropped it. Until the next incurable case we had come across. A surge of incurable diseases showed up on our doorstep, and each time someone died, Axilya had reminded me that I could've saved them.

One day, it had become too much, and something snapped. I left when she was asleep, swearing to never work with her again. It didn't stop her from disparaging my name across the continent until nearly every town took one look at me before chasing me away.

I handed her a vial as she asked and pushed down the memories that haunted me. Her slender hands were careful and precise. She clipped a petal, leaving the rest intact. Potions and antidotes were not easy to create. The first hundred attempts often failed. Sometimes the failure had no effect on the patient. Sometimes it led to a faster death than the patient otherwise would've had.

There were ten bleeding heart lilies to work with—only one of the rare variants that had once been a tale told over fires. And as the days dragged by, Nyri was getting weaker, barely a pulse left. My fangs were aware of the blood struggling to pump through her body as her organs shut down one by one. My tonics fought the symptoms enough to give her a little more time, but they had grown less effective.

Thoughts of turning her lingered in the back of my mind.

If the bleeding heart lily didn't work...

If we were too late with the cure...

An oath to never change the unwilling wrapped itself around my morals, but each day that passed in failure loosened the grip that oath had on my heart.

Axilya had created a healing salve using the delicate white petals—better than any I had ever seen before. She created a tonic that warmed my blood and gave me energy thicker than any blood. But all of our previous attempts hadn't so much as made Nyri stir. Most of the flowers had been used, which meant they were running out of attempts.

"You're not doing it right," Tareen said. She had been making a suspicious number of visits to the infirmary since we started working on the tonic. For the most part, she had stayed out of the way, taking her breathing treatments or pretending to look at the collection on my walls, but her presence lingered.

"And what do you know?" Axilya raised her brow at the witch. She wasn't used to being challenged.

"I know plenty about potion making, and I know you're doing it wrong. You are heating the petals too quickly." Tareen pulled at her fingers.

"I have been making healing tonics for over two centuries. Do you honestly think you know better than me?" Axilya liked being the smartest in the room—she often was—but Tareen didn't back down.

"You may be skilled with regular herbs, but it's clear you haven't dealt with magical plants before. Move, and I'll show you how it's done." Tareen didn't wait for the nymph to answer before sliding her way into the work station.

I stepped between the witch and the nymph to avoid any arguments. "I'll help."

Tareen waved her hand, lowering the heat of the flame. She dumped out what Axilya started. The witch worked with deft hands, tearing apart the purple variant of the flower. It made me nervous watching her work since there were few flowers left, and she claimed she couldn't make healing potions. Despite that, she moved with focused confidence.

"I'll be elsewhere if you need me." Axilya huffed as she left the room.

"What's her problem?" Tareen asked.

I held back my smile. I shouldn't have been pleased by my former mentor's frustration. "Don't mind her."

Tareen shrugged and went back to work, mixing various ingredients I wouldn't have thought of trying. Hours passed by, and at the end of it, we had a small vial filled with a lavender liquid. Tareen held it up to the light, inspecting it for a long moment.

"If anything is going to save your friend, it's this." She pressed the glass into my hands, and her hands lingered.

My throat tightened, hope bubbling up in intense waves. I held the vial in my hands, hoping Tareen had been able to do what I hadn't.

The bodies in the room made me nervous. Zathrian's eyes were sunken in and dark as he watched my every move. Aukina held Reamann's hand a few feet behind me. The hope and desperation coming off the mermaid made sweat collect on my brow. Viridian watched from the shadows, mostly hidden, but I could feel his gaze burning into me. Tareen sat in a chair to the side, rocking as she watched. Even if healing wasn't her specialty, she wanted to see if her concoction worked.

It wasn't necessary to have everyone gathered. I had told them all as much, but it hadn't stopped them from insisting.

"It won't work instantly," I said, making sure their expectations didn't get too high. If Tareen had done what others had failed to, Nyri would wake up, but it wouldn't have been immediate.

Her body had suffered for two weeks. That kind of damage rarely healed instantaneously.

No one responded to me, making the sweat on the back of my neck lick the curls of my hair. That was why I preferred to keep my hair short, but in the chaos of the past few weeks, I hadn't made it to the one hair stylist at the estate.

Nyri had grown pale compared to the tan she had slowly gained working in the garden. There was barely any color left in her skin. She had lost weight as well.

"Help me prop her up." I met Zathrian's eyes. He was next to Nyri a split second later, holding her up. His fingers brushed against her hair with the care of a lover who would do anything to save the one he loved.

I pulled the cork of the vial off and held it up to her lips. I poured a little at a time, careful not to make her choke on the liquid. I emptied every last drop into her mouth. The silence in the room thickened as everyone waited for a miracle. Even I fell into the trap of hope, half-expecting Nyri to open her eyes and smile with a joy too few had in this world.

When nothing happened, I said, "It'll take time."

The room let out a collective breath. Only the demon king continued to hold still, hoping, praying to whatever higher power he believed in.

At first, everyone settled in, ready to wait, but one by one people left, disappointed by the lack of immediate response. Tareen was the first to leave, slinking out without a word. Aukina and Reamann slipped out next, muttering something about needing to get back to their jobs. I was sure the kitchen and the guardsmen could spare the two of them for a day, but I didn't question them. The heaviness in the room made it difficult to do anything other than wait for Nyri to open her eyes, something none of us knew would happen.

I hadn't noticed when Viridian left. I was sure he had to attend to the estate to ensure it was running smoothly, even as the weight of the looming death of the demon king's mate hung in a heavy layer over the entire estate.

I was intent on staying all night, but there was a pull in my chest, calling out to me. Zathrian would stay by her side until she either woke up or passed away. The thought pulled up emotions I had shoved into the dredges.

"I'm going to get some air," I said, keeping my voice soft.

Either Zathrian didn't hear me, or he didn't have the energy to answer.

I slipped out of the large black doors of the demon king's room and went straight to the staircase, climbing higher and higher until I made it to the roof. Astoria stood on the edge of the wall with her hands clasped behind her back. She looked out among the forest, the chilly breeze ruffling the waves of her hair.

"If the tonic doesn't work, I don't think Nyri will make it until morning," I said.

"She won't." Her voice whispered through the wind, a confirmation more chilling than the night air. "I feel her soul slipping away, calling out for help."

My hands shook, my composure threatening to come undone. I had kept it together long enough to search for a solution. There was nothing else I could do except wait. "If she dies, what do I do?" My voice cracked as the walls built around my heart crumbled.

Astoria was in front of me a moment later, steadying my hands. "You move on, just as the rest of the world will. But you hold onto her memory, even if the rest of the world forgets."

Tears slid down my face. "I fucking hate death. I'm so damned tired of it. I don't understand how you do it."

Astoria pushed my bangs out of the way and placed a gentle kiss on my brow. "I want to tell you that it gets easier. I suppose for some it does. They build a numbness to it. I never want to slip into that mindset, because it's a dangerous place to be. Instead, I take the pain and focus on the living, on the joy that mortals find while they can. It... helps."

I let myself fall into the reaper, my face resting against her plush chest. Tears slid down my face as I finally allowed myself to feel the pain and fear that I had been pushing back since Nyri fell ill—since before that. Astoria held me close, her warmth shielding me from the worst of it. Even if I lost Nyri, there were reasons to go on. I couldn't leave behind Aukina, and the residents of Ethlow needed me. Then there was Astoria. A grim reaper who had swept me off my feet unexpectedly.

"I'm just afraid I'll lose myself if I lose her," I admitted when the tears began to slow.

"I won't let that—" Astoria's body tensed. She lowered her voice as she said, "Get inside. Now."

I pulled back, trying to figure out her sudden change in tone. I looked around, even as Astoria shoved me back. My vampiric instincts kept me on my feet, but as a dark figure emerged from the shadows, my knees wobbled.

"I'm a little surprised to find you here with a vampire no less, Astoria. Did you find yourself a little plaything while hunting me down?"

Chapter 26

Astoria spun around, her scythe appearing in her hands. She placed herself between the stranger and me.

"Lonis." Venom dripped from her mouth, and the air charged with power.

The man Astoria called Lonis jumped from the wall and floated down to the floor. His own scythe rested on his shoulders, the sharp black blade curling to his side. The air became acrid with strange powers—ones that resembled Astoria's.

He kept his distance between him and Astoria, as if he knew better than to taunt the reaper. "You never should've followed me. This is above your head."

Astoria twisted her scythe in her hands, angling it threateningly. "No, Lonis. This is above yours. You know better than all of us that reapers have to uphold the sacred oath. You know the destruction that will rain down if we turn away from our responsibilities."

Lonis stepped to the side, allowing him to look at me directly. His gaze was of a predator ready to pounce. He licked his lips as he looked me up and down. "Aren't you the one shirking your responsibilities? It seems you found yourself a plaything. Maybe

I should take a bite." He clicked his teeth together, pretending to bite the air.

Disgust twisted my gut at the male's gaze. I stretched my fingers, readying my claws to defend. I was aware the power electrifying the air was beyond my skills. I wasn't a fighter, and even my vampiric strength wasn't enough to face a reaper and win. Yet, I refused to back down. I instantly knew this was the man who poisoned Nyri and nearly killed Viridian.

Astoria spun like a tornado, weaving her scythe for Lonis' throat. He disappeared before the blade made contact. The air buzzed, and I spun, poised to strike, but it was too late. A yellow light flashed from my pocket, and then there was a blade hovering in front of my throat. The cool metal burned with darkness. It wouldn't take much for Lonis to slit my throat, but he'd have to behead me and burn me to stop my body from regenerating.

"Don't—" Astoria started to snarl.

"Don't what?" Lonis taunted. "Make any move and your lover is dead."

I huffed. "What's up with you and threatening people's partners? Are you so pathetic that you have to go for someone weaker to feel like you have any power over the world?"

"Satella, careful." Astoria's words were a tight warning. I was sure her face held the same mask it did most of the time, but her voice lacked the whimsical nature I had grown to love.

"I could make you bend to your knees," Lonis snarled.

"What is it with males and the obsession of getting a woman on her knees?" I asked. I knew I was playing a dangerous game, but I wasn't about to cower. Not when I could distract him enough for Astoria to make a move. "Is it because you know I'm better than you, so you want me below you, because I promise you couldn't handle this." I flashed my teeth, hoping he'd take me more seriously.

Lonis tilted his head. "I thought you would quake in my presence."

Fear twisted in my core as I felt death emanating from him. It was different from Astoria. Her presence was warm and comforting, one that was easy to fall into. Lonis was like death himself. Darkness poured out from him, but it was different from the darkness in me. It had twisted and mutated with anger and hatred.

"I'm not afraid of death." It was an utter lie, but I held my head up. "And I'm not afraid of you." I was grateful I didn't have a heartbeat to give away the terror flooding my system.

"Just because you're immortal, it doesn't mean you can't die." Lonis' eyes danced with glee. He was the type who liked to play with his hunt before he made the kill. I couldn't imagine how someone like him had become a grim reaper, but I knew nothing about the origin of grim reapers.

"Then I'm not truly immortal," I said. "Perhaps I'm just long-lived. If it's my time, I'll accept it, if it means you get what you deserve for poisoning my friend." *Shit.* I wasn't ready to die. I hoped Astoria was doing something while I distracted the reaper, but I couldn't hear her, even with my vampiric senses.

"I could find out for you." He moved the scythe closer to my neck, the cold metal brushing against my throat as a whispered threat.

Panic bubbled in my chest. I should've run when Astoria told me, but confusion had made me hesitate.

"I thought grim reapers were supposed to comfort souls on their journey to the underworld," I barely managed to croak. My cool exterior was breaking. I wouldn't be able to hold it together any longer. "When did you take to killing?"

"When I was shown a better world." Lonis grinned, flashing sharp rotten teeth. The scent that came from his mouth made me gag. I started to take a step back out of instinct, but Lonis' gravelly voice halted me. "One move, and I'll slice your head off your body."

"I don't think so," Viridian said, a whisper in my ear.

Shadows wrapped around me, and the world went dark. It was the same darkness that had called to me once before. Teal eyes cut through the darkness. A cool hand grabbed mine, and then I was flying. The world reappeared as my back hit the stone wall, opposite to where I had been standing a moment prior.

"Don't move," Viridian ordered. The power lacing his voice snapped my bones into place.

Viridian slipped through the shadows, appearing behind Lonis—Astoria was nowhere to be seen. The demon grabbed a black dagger from the abyss and shoved it between Lonis' ribs, shadows ripping the skin where the blade pierced.

The reaper disappeared, slipping away from Viridian's grip. When he reappeared, he stood on the stone wall, holding Viridian's dagger. "Didn't get enough of me last time, huh?"

Viridian bared his mouth full of sharp teeth, his eyes glowing brighter than they ever had before. "As long as you pose a threat to the sire, you will be my enemy."

"The sire?" Lonis mused. "Why do you treat him with respect when you know you are more powerful than him?"

The five demon rulers of the lands were the most powerful beings in the mortal realms—or so the stories said. Viridian served Zathrian. He wouldn't do that if what Lonis said was true. Yet, Viridian didn't flinch.

"I'm not interested in talking." The demon pulled out another dagger ablaze in shadows, and when he flicked his wrist, the blade split in two. He tossed it, but Lonis disappeared well before the knives hit their mark. Viridian appeared where Lonis had been, catching the blades before they flew into the unknown.

Lonis emerged from hiding and flung Viridian's sacrificed dagger, but he didn't aim it at the demon. The blade flew towards me. I twisted out of the way and the dagger thunked into the wall.

"You're going to regret that," Viridian said. His shadows raged around him, even as he held still.

"And what are you going to do about it? You can't even hit me. You should know that by now." Lonis cackled, power surging through his veins.

Viridian smiled, joy dancing in his eyes like I had never seen before. He twisted a new dagger in his hand, but he didn't move to attack. He didn't have to.

Astoria flipped out of the air, swinging her scythe down with precision. Lonis barely had time to react, but he moved enough to stop the weapon from cleaving through his chest. Instead, it ripped through his arm, and black blood spattered against the wall.

"You bitch," he growled. His own scythe was in his hand a moment later. He swung it at Astoria, but her lithe body twisted with grace that left me in awe.

"Leave while you can." Astoria's power surged, a commanding aura that could make the human race fall to their knees and worship her.

"This is none of your business, Astoria." Lonis' face twisted into a feral mask. His killing intent made the air too thick to breathe.

I glanced at the door, wondering if there was a way to slip inside the estate without being noticed, but I feared any movement would bring attention to me. I wasn't sure if getting inside would help against a being that could move through the folds of space and appear wherever they wished.

"You attacked Satella, making this very much my business." Astoria winked from view and appeared mid-action as she swung her foot, knocking Lonis' feet out from him.

As the reaper fell, Viridian tossed a dagger into his chest, hitting his mark with impressive precision. Astoria held her scythe over Lonis' neck.

"Give up now," she warned. "Go back to whatever hole you crawled out of, and I'll consider forgiving you." The venom in her voice held no room for forgiveness. Lonis could crawl on his knees and beg, but it wouldn't make a difference. Astoria was a woman scorned, and she'd never forget the affront against her.

"You don't understand." Lonis laughed, quickly looking more deranged. "This is above you or me. This is above immortal vampires and pesky mortal souls."

"Enough!" Astoria snapped. She swung her blade down, but she stopped when Lonis uttered his last statement.

"The demon rule is coming to an end," Lonis said, his eyes glowing with wild delight.

Viridian stepped out of the shadows, his face hard. "What do you mean?"

"Maybe you would know, Shadow Slinger, if you hadn't settled as a servant for a lesser demon." Lonis smirked, delighting in the frustration of the others.

Viridian stepped forward, two curved daggers in his hands. "If you don't—"

Lonis disappeared before he finished his sentence. I felt the brush of death before Lonis appeared in front of me, already swinging his scythe. I tried to move, but I couldn't match his pace.

Astoria's scream filled my ears as my own panic flooded my system, but there was nothing I could do. There was no time to brace myself for the attack.

The blade was nearly upon me, but my vision flooded with pink and purple.

Astoria grunted, dropping her scythe to the ground as Lonis' weapon went through her chest. Her black blood sprayed against my face. She fell to her knees, and blood quickly pooled around her.

No. No. No. Fuck. Fuck.

Chapter 27

I scrambled to Astoria as Lonis' cackle filled my ears.

"This is even better than I hoped," Lonis purred. "I was expecting to collect the soul of a vampire, but I didn't think you were stupid enough to sacrifice yourself for someone of the mortal realm."

Astoria coughed, blood leaking from her mouth. "It is our job to protect the souls of the living. No matter the cost. Satella is not part of your scheme."

Lonis twisted his scythe, making Astoria groan in pain. "Too bad your sacrifice is in vain, because once I'm done with you, I'm going to kill the vampire."

Astoria laughed. "Just tell me. Why use poison on the demon king's mate when you could've sliced her like this?"

Lonis leaned and whispered, but not quietly enough to stop me from hearing, "Because I wanted to start a war. I don't care if the pathetic human dies."

"Too bad you failed." Viridian stood behind Lonis with Astoria's scythe in his hands, posed to strike. He swung with incredible strength and speed. Lonis wasn't able to utter a single word before his head was cleaved off. His skull hit the ground with a *crack!* Blood sprayed, mixing with Astoria's.

The grim reaper's body began to collapse, but before it hit the ground, it disintegrated into shadows.

"You took the killing blow from me," Astoria said, struggling to spit out the words.

Viridian let the scythe fall, but before it clattered to the ground, it disappeared. "You were too slow."

Astoria laughed, which quickly turned to coughing.

I scrambled to her front, looking at her torn-up skin. My hands shook. "Don't move. We need to seal the wound."

Astoria grabbed my hand, but her grip was weak. "Don't bother."

"If we don't get you help, you'll—" I couldn't finish my statement.

"I'll be fine." She coughed again, more blood leaking from her mouth. It was impossible to believe as I watched her fade from my eyes.

"I have salves to stop the bleeding. If we get you to the infirmary, I can save you. I saved Viridian." I looked at the demon who hovered nearby, saying nothing. "Help me move her." I could carry her to the infirmary, but I didn't have that kind of time. I needed Viridian to use his shadows to move us quickly. I saved Viridian. I could save her.

"Satella." Astoria's voice was firm, even with her shallow breath. I looked back at her, the emerald color in her eyes fading. "I accept my fate."

"I don't," I snapped. Astoria had brought me back to life. She reminded me what it was like to step outside the halls of Ethlow. She made me feel like I deserved to be loved for the first time since I had become a vampire. I couldn't lose her, especially with Nyri on her deathbed.

"I'm just happy I got to spend time with you." Astoria stroked my cheek.

Tears slid down my face. I hated her acceptance. I wanted to pull her closer, but the weapon stopped me. "Why did you do that for me? Why did you sacrifice yourself for a soulless vampire like me?"

"Because I love you," Astoria said. Her eyes sparkled with joy, even as she faded.

"I don't deserve your love." I couldn't stop the steady stream of tears.

"Everyone deserves to be loved, especially someone as special as you." A coughing fit made her body jolt. "Help me take this out of my body."

"You'll bleed out," I whispered.

"Satella. Please." I wanted to fight her. I wanted to drag her to the infirmary and perform a miracle, but as she tugged at the weapon, I knew I had to help her.

Astoria winced as I pulled the blade out. Blood gushed from the open wound. I pulled her against me, hoping I could slow the bleeding. "Please don't leave me."

"You'll be okay," Astoria whispered. "And we'll meet again."

I held her close to me. Her body went limp in my arms, and panic flooded my system. "No, no, no," I sobbed. "I love you. Please stay with me."

But she didn't respond. I was too late. She didn't hear me tell her how I really felt.

Her body faded in my arms, leaving nothing behind but the blood soaking my clothes. I curled into myself, a sob ripping through my soul. I hated death.

I *fucking* hated death.

I didn't know how long I cried on the roof, but when there was nothing left inside of me, I slowly sat up. Viridian stood in the shadows. He hadn't moved, watching me fall apart.

I would've felt embarrassed, but there was nothing left for me to feel. I was numb and broken. I pulled myself off the ground, knowing I couldn't stand there all night. I looked at Viridian and hated him for the pity on his face.

"Don't say anything," I said with icy rage. There was nothing the demon could say or do that wouldn't make me hate his very being.

Viridian held still, keeping his lips sealed. The only indication that he had heard me was the flicker in his eyes.

I dragged myself inside, needing to wash the blood off me before I slipped into a darkness I couldn't escape. Viridian said nothing as I left him to clean up the mess on the roof.

No amount of water made me feel clean. It was as if Astoria's blood permanently stained my skin. I scrubbed and scrubbed until my skin was raw. Then I kept scrubbing. I wouldn't have stopped if there hadn't been a panicked knock on my door.

The water sloshed as I stepped out of the tub, not caring about the water spilling onto the ground. I threw on the first clean clothes I could find. It was easier to slip on the mask I had worn as a healer as the desperation on the other side put me into work mode. My personal problems didn't matter when others needed me.

I threw the door open, water dripping from my hair. Aukina stood wide-eyed on the other side. I scanned her for injuries out of habit, but she looked fine, other than her red eyes and nose.

"Come quick!" She grabbed my hand and dragged me out of the room before I could put on any shoes.

The darkness flickered at the edges of my vision. There was only one reason Aukina would drag me through the estate with that much urgency.

Nyri.

If she was dead, I didn't know what I'd do. I had already lost Astoria.

Nyri's death would wreck what was left of me.

As we approached the demon king's doors, I resisted Aukina's pull. The gold inlets in the black door seemed to swirl, taunting me for what lay inside.

Aukina paused long enough to look at me. She smiled and squeezed my hand. "It's okay."

Her words sounded as if they were coming from underwater. I couldn't believe everything was okay when nothing felt okay.

The mermaid tugged on my arm, refusing to let me fall into the darkness. As we entered the demon king's door, Zathrian's soft sobs hit my ears. If Aukina hadn't been holding my hand, I would've turned and ran until the shadows consumed me.

"I heard I have you to thank for my life," Nyri whispered. "As well as Tareen."

I blinked, deep blue eyes meeting mine.

Something broke inside of me. I threw myself onto the bed and wrapped my arms around Nyri. Sobs wracked my body as I clung to my friend.

Nyri stroked my hair, comforting as new emotions broke through. My mask shattered, and every emotion I had been biting back and so much more came pouring out.

"I'm okay," she whispered, holding me close and letting me cry on her. I should've been the one comforting her, since she had nearly died, but I couldn't put myself together.

Grief lifted from the air as Nyri smiled. She brought back the joy that had been void for weeks.

"So, tell me what's been going on while I've been out," Nyri asked.

I bit my tongue. Now wasn't the time to tell her or anyone else what happened to Astoria. Nyri waking up was a celebration, not a place for deep sorrow.

So I let Aukina go on about the training class Reamann and she ran, and how Wistari had become good at kicking other warriors' asses. She told her about a new recipe that she made, and a date Reamann had taken her own. She talked about Tareen joining us for food and how the witch was essential to finding a cure for her.

Then Zathrian stepped up and told her about some meeting he had to attend other things I didn't care about. While they were distracted, I slipped out of the room, knowing if the attention was put on me, I'd only bring the mood down. The others could have Nyri. As long as she was alive, I was satisfied.

Chapter 28

Flowers decorated every inch of Ethlow in celebration. I had never seen that many flowers in one place before, but Zathrian didn't spare any expense for the party. After weeks of a deep gloom looming over the estate, a celebration was needed to lift the remaining despair.

Only it wouldn't lift the loss of Astoria, but that was a heaviness that was only in my heart. I hadn't told anyone else what went down on the roof while Nyri was waking up.

Everywhere I went, I expected to see the purple and pink hair of the reaper. It had been a week since that night, but there was a part of me that didn't want to believe it was real. Astoria had flipped into my life too recently to disappear like that, but the ache in my chest told me it was real.

The estate was flooded with preparations for Nyri's party. Aukina had been in the kitchen all morning preparing tarts of savory and sweet nature as well as every other kind of food imaginable. There hadn't been a party this grand since before my arrival at the estate, which left everyone buzzing with excitement.

I wondered if that same excitement would have been there if they knew the truth of the sacrifice made. To save me and to stop Lonis, a bright soul winked out of existence.

I had never thought about a grim reaper dying. It didn't make sense, but one of Tareen's books explained that the scythe of a grim reaper had the power to rip a soul away from its body, and few were immune to its powers. It explained how Viridian nearly died. A powerful demon could barely take down a grim reaper without the sacrifice of another.

"Is that what you're wearing to the party?" Tareen's voice called out to me.

I spun, my deep red dress flaring at the bottom. "It's one of my nicest dresses."

Tareen looked me up and down. "You look hot."

"Ew, don't say that." It was easier to slip into playful banter than I had anticipated. A century of wearing a mask made it easy to slip it back on, even as the corruption inside my soul had grown more intense.

"Seriously, if I had a body like yours, I'd flaunt it," Tareen said. She patted her round belly. "Nobody likes people with a body like mine."

I grimaced at the witch. "You are fucking adorable. Don't say stuff like that."

"I'm just surprised you're still single. That's all."

I knew the witch meant well, but I couldn't hide my wince. "The last person I loved died."

Tareen blinked. "Oh." A moment of silence flooded between us. "I'm sorry."

I did my best to smile. "It's okay." It wasn't, but I didn't feel like getting into it. "Let's head to the party."

Music of stringed instruments filled the grand hall of Ethlow. The lights were dimmed as people swayed on the dance floor. In the center of it all, Zathrian held Nyri in his arms, spinning her around and looking at her as if she was the only one in the crowded room. Onlookers gawked at the site. It was strange seeing the demon king with his horns and tail spinning a human around.

The estate was well aware of their relationship, but they rarely paraded around together, let alone danced under sparkling lights in stunning outfits.

Color stained Nyri's cheeks, making her look utterly alive. Her recovery had taken less than a day after she drank the tonic of the bleeding heart lily. I had never seen someone fully recover that quickly from a poison that nearly killed them. If I could recreate the tonic, it would change the way I practiced medicine. I was grateful Tareen was the one who had figured it out—not Axilya.

The nymph had left the moment she found out the demon king's mate had woken up.

"She looks so happy," Aukina said. She held Reamann's hand, smiling brightly.

"She does," I agreed.

"You don't," Reamann said.

I snapped my head on the verge of snarling at the demon guardsman. "Excuse me?"

"I just meant you look like there's something bothering you. Did something happen?" The genuine tone he used threw me off. I was used to bickering and jabs.

My instincts told me to insult him and tell him he was stupid, but he was the only one who seemed to see right through my mask. "I can't talk about it," I whispered. I wasn't forbidden to speak about the incident on the roof. I hadn't seen Viridian since, so he hadn't had the chance to tell me to keep it a secret. But I had decided on my own that my friends didn't need to worry about grim reapers attacking innocents.

And I knew I couldn't physically talk about it without breaking down.

"You should come to our self-defense class. It's good to work out difficult emotions," Reamann said. He didn't prod me to say more, which I appreciated.

"I'll think about it. I don't know if it's worth messing up my nails." I looked down at my fingers painted in a purple and pink ombre. I had Elcy change them for me, even though it hurt to look at them.

Reamann twisted his face, but before he could say anything, Aukina pulled him out to the dance floor. "Come on. I want to see how good you are on your feet, since I already know how good you are off them."

Tareen shook her head. "Disgusting, isn't it?"

I bit back my chuckle. It was clear the witch wanted that kind of relationship. I knew that feeling too well, but I wasn't sure if I wanted to put myself out there again. "I think it's cute. They found each other in a place meant for rejects."

Tareen pressed her lips into a tight line. She acted as if she was fine by herself, but I saw through her act.

"Are you going to dance?" I asked.

"Don't know yet. Are you?"

"No." The thought of dancing tore me apart as I thought about how much Astoria would have loved the music. She danced when there was silence. I could only imagine how much she would've spun me around if she were here. "But you should. You'll have fun, and maybe you'll meet the one out there."

"Doubtful," Tareen said. "I know *the one* doesn't live at Ethlow. If they did, I would already know."

I didn't say anything, understanding that feeling. What Aukina and Reamann found, and what Nyri and Zathrian found seemed rare in the estate. But maybe it wasn't as rare as I thought.

"I think I will dance," Tareen said. She pulled at her fingers, fear and excitement mixing together. "See you tomorrow for dinner?" The question was filled with hope. Was she still allowed to eat with us now that Nyri was back?

"See you tomorrow," I confirmed.

Tareen smiled brightly before slipping onto the dance floor. Her black dress stood out among the colors of the residents, but her joy matched theirs. It felt as if there was something changing within the demon king's estate, bringing happiness that had been lacking for decades.

I played with the crow's gifted ring in my pocket. From the outside, it looked like a simple piece of jewelry, but it felt like so much more. A gift from a crow who had been a grim reaper's friend.

My chest ached as blissful faces danced in front of me. I slipped away from the party, knowing I didn't belong at the celebration. I was happy Nyri survived. I didn't know what would have become of me if the tonic hadn't worked, but I could only hide the hole in my heart for so long.

My room was quiet. I had been avoiding it as much as possible, not wanting to linger anywhere that reminded me of Astoria. But the rainbow hornworms had gone into chrysalis form, and I was expecting them to emerge any day. Focusing on their lives helped the days drag a little less.

When I leaned in to inspect my babies, I noticed one of the cocoons wiggling. Afternoon Tea was attempting to break free. The shell split with the bug's attempt, and it wiggled out. Its wings glimmered with the colors of the rainbow, but they were damp from the cocoon.

Afternoon Tea shook its body, and tears pricked my eyes. He had triumphed in his transformation, and I wasn't about to take away his freedom. I scooped him up carefully and carried him outside. It was near sunset, but there was enough time to release the rainbow moth into the wild. As much as I would've loved to keep him pinned on my wall after his life cycle came to an end, I didn't want to keep him trapped. I wanted Afternoon Tea to live a full life, what little life a bug like him had.

I barely paid attention to my surroundings, looking at Afternoon Tea instead. He had only been with me for a short time, but I loved him.

Which was why it was time to let him go. I held out my hand and waited for his wings to dry and spread. Slowly, he tested out his wings. He crawled to the tip of my finger before taking off. I watched as the fading sun glittered against his design, showing his full beauty. I waited until I couldn't see him anymore before I turned to head back to the estate.

I took a single step before a rope snapped around my ankle. My leg was yanked from beneath me, and the world flipped upside down as the rope pulled higher. I pulled at my dress as it threatened to fall above my head. I yelped in pain and confusion, but when green eyes met mine, I froze.

"You're a little too easy to trap," Astoria said, leaning forward with her hands clasped behind her back. "You need to be careful, or the wrong person will take advantage of you."

Blood rushed to my face, and I couldn't think. "Astoria." I hadn't spoken her name since she faded from my arms.

"The one and only," she chirped, as if she had never been stabbed and killed.

"How? I don't understand. You died." Despite her standing in front of me, I didn't believe it.

"I told you I was fine, didn't I?" She tapped my nose.

I wanted to cry and scream. "I thought you were lying to comfort me."

"I have never lied to you," Astoria said, her face softening into something more serious.

"Get me down." My voice shook as my shock wore off. I couldn't stand to be hanging upside down for a second longer.

Astoria grabbed her scythe from thin air before slicing the rope tied around my ankle. Before I could twist and land on my feet, the grim reaper caught me in her arms. Her warmth surrounded me, making it feel real. A sob caught in my throat.

"I saw you die," I whispered.

"Did you think I would go down that easily? It takes a lot more than that to kill a grim reaper." She lowered my feet to the ground, but she didn't take her hands off me.

"Then does that mean Lonis is out there?" The thought sent ice through my veins.

"Somewhere, but I don't think he'll mess with Ethlow again."

I nodded slowly, but I wasn't convinced. It was clear Lonis was working for someone. If he didn't come back himself, I was sure others would come. I didn't want to focus on that, though. Not when Astoria was back.

"Where have you been?" The thought of Astoria intentionally staying away while I suffered thinking she was dead was unbearable.

She ran her fingers through my hair. "It took time to regenerate, but I came as soon as I could."

"I thought you were dead." I didn't know why I was repeating this.

Astoria cupped the back of my neck and pulled me into a kiss. "I'm not going anywhere. I'm yours in life and death."

Chapter 29

"They're waiting for us," I whispered between kisses.

"Uh-huh." Astoria slipped her tongue into my mouth, and I arched my back.

"We should go," I whispered, pulling back.

Astoria pushed her bottom lip out, pouting. It made me want to stay locked in my room with her for the rest of the day. But we had time for that later. "They'll eat without us. Come on."

"They can eat without us, if it means I get to eat you."

My thighs clenched at the suggestion, but I resisted her temptation. I pulled the reaper out of my room and into the garden. The others were already sitting in the grass, waiting for us. They had several blankets set out in the green grass beneath the reds, oranges, and yellows decorating the trees above. I was sure the grass was only green because of Nyri's magic touch, and it made me smile.

Aukina sat on a blanket with Reamann, while Nyri sat with Zathrian. Tareen had her own blanket with several books sitting next to her. I pulled Astoria next to me as we reached the picnic. She shifted on her feet nervously, which was strange to see from her.

"Everyone." I paused for the others to look at us. "This is Astoria. My girlfriend."

Nyri scrambled to her feet. She wiped her hand on her pants before holding it out to Astoria. "I'm Nyri. I've been looking forward to meeting you. I can't believe Satella kept you hidden for so long."

The reaper took Nyri's hand and kissed the back of it. "I'd say it's because she's embarrassed, but I think she just wanted to keep me between her legs a little longer." Astoria winked at Nyri, making her giggle.

I felt the color rush to my cheeks. "Astoria," I snapped, but she only winked at me.

"It's really nice to meet you," Aukina said, quickly changing the subject. "I don't know if you eat, but I brought a variety of food." She gestured to the spread before her.

"This is lovely." Astoria grabbed a strawberry and popped it into her mouth.

"So you're the grim reaper who's been running around my estate," Zathrian said.

I froze, realizing Viridian hadn't told the demon king what happened on the roof or who poisoned Nyri. I waited, unsure if Astoria would correct him or say anything. I didn't know if it was better if she stayed silent or not.

"Guilty," Astoria said. "The place has really changed since the last time I was here. Everyone is... happier." She squeezed my hand and looked at me, but I found myself watching the demon king.

There hadn't been a death since his last lover met an unfortunate fate. His face faltered, a shadow flashing over his eyes. Nyri placed her hand on his shoulder, and he looked at her. For a moment, I feared the mood would sour from the topic, but when Zathrian looked back at Astoria, there was a smile on his face.

"It's all thanks to Nyri. She has reminded me it's okay to be happy." He kissed her temple, and Nyri blushed. The king had come too close to losing her, and I feared what that would have meant for the estate. Nyri had the shortest lifespan out of the group, and it was only a matter of time before she died one way or another.

"She seems to be special." Astoria dropped to the ground, crossing her legs as she settled into a seated position.

"She is."

Astoria leaned in and lowered her voice, but my ears picked it up with my enhanced senses. "And Leira approves."

Zathrian's body went taut at the mention of his former lover. He swallowed hard as a flood of emotions moved through him at the mention of his late partner.

"So will you be sticking around for a while?" Tareen asked, bringing the change of subject that was needed.

I sat next to Astoria, unsure of what she'd say.

"I'll be here as much as I can be, but it'll depend on the state of the rest of the world." Astoria's answer was more than I could ask for. I loved her, and I loved having her around. Whatever time I got with her, I'd be grateful for.

We fell into a comfortable rhythm of talking, laughing, and eating, and the world felt right, even as I knew there were dangers lurking around the corner. It made it easier to treasure every moment I had with Astoria and the rest of my friends. I rested my head on her lap, and she casually stroked her fingers through my hair. Everything about the moment was perfect, and I committed the laughter to memory for any dark days in the future.

As long as I had those I loved by my side, I knew I could get through whatever lay ahead.

"That's so pretty!" Aukina called out, pointing to the sky.

The rest of us followed her gaze. Colorful wings flapped above us, and I instantly knew it was Afternoon Tea. I held up my hand, and he landed on my finger. After being released, he came back to check on me, making my heart swell with joy.

"Hello there, friend."

Author's Note

Thank you so much for taking time to read my book! If you've made it this far, I would greatly appreciate it if you took the time to leave a review on Amazon/Goodreads. As an indie author, reviews are essential for gaining more visibility. All reviews are appreciated! If you ever have any questions, concerns, or general comments, please feel free to reach out to me directly at evereri.theauthor@gmail.com!

ALSO BY EVERERI

Read more in The Demons of Kinzlea

The Demon King's Pet
The Demon King's Cook
The Demon King's Healer
The Demon King's Librarian
The Demon King's Teacher
The Demon King's Assassin

Coming Soon!

The Demon Queen's Rise
Coming in early 2025

The Unfortunate Fate of Mates

Available on the Dreame App:

The Four Beta Brothers
The Stolen Wolf Princess
The Long Lost Luna
The Unwanted Wolf
The Blood Moon Twins

Acknowledgements

To my friends who constantly remind me why I love writing. When things get difficult, and I start questioning why I bother, you remind me of my passion. Things haven't always been easy, but I'm lucky to have friends like you. I don't know where I'd be without any of you. Your support means the world to me, and I love you all to the end of time.

Special thanks to Sam, who inspired Satella. You are one of my favorite "readers." I love our late night talks. You are incredible in so many ways, and I never want you to forget that.

ABOUT THE AUTHOR

EverEri is a lover of romance, fantasy, and fairytales, and one of her favorite things to do is to bring a story and characters alive through the written word. EverEri began her true writing journey in the paranormal romance world in 2021, and she never plans to turn back. Whether it's demons, dragons, werewolves, merfolk, or other magical beings, she plans to bring her passions to life in each book she writes.

Want to see more?

Follow EverEri on social media:

IG: everlastingeri

Tik Tok: author_evereri

FB: EverEri's Reading Group

Newsletter: evereri.theauthor@gmail.com

www.ingramcontent.com/pod-product-compliance
Lightning Source LLC
Chambersburg PA
CBHW030306180626
46810CB00003B/934